THE BELIAL RECRUIT

Book 4 of the Belial Series

R.D. Brady

BOOKS BY R.D. BRADY

Hominid

The Belial Series (in order)
The Belial Stone
The Belial Library
The Belial Ring
Recruit: A Belial Series Novella
The Belial Children
The Belial Origins
The Belial Search
The Belial Guard
The Belial Warrior
The Belial Plan
The Belial Witches
The Belial War
The Belial Fall
The Belial Sacrifice

The Belial Rebirth Series
The Belial Rebirth
The Belial Spear

The Belial Restored
The Belial Blood
The Belial Angel
The Belial Templar (Coming Soon)

The A.L.I.V.E. Series
B.E.G.I.N.
A.L.I.V.E.
D.E.A.D.
R.I.S.E.
S.A.V.E.

The H.A.L.T. Series
Into the Cage
Into the Dark *(Coming soon)*

The Steve Kane Series
Runs Deep
Runs Deeper

The Unwelcome Series
Protect
Seek
Proxy

The Nola James Series
Surrender the Fear
Escape the Fear
Tackle the Fear
Return the Fear

The Gates of Artemis Series
The Key of Apollo
The Curse of Hecate
The Return of the Gods

R.D. BRADY WRITING AS SADIE HOBBES

The Demon Cursed Series
    Demon Cursed
    Demon Revealed
    Demon Heir

The Four Kingdoms
    Order of the Goddess

Be sure to sign up for R.D.'s mailing list to be the first to hear when she has a new release!

"Courage is the decision that there is something more important than the fear we feel."
The Essential Edgar Cayce, 27

CHAPTER 1

DETROIT, MICHIGAN

Fifteen-year old Lou Thomas walked down the street, her shoulders hunched against the cold. She knew there were two of them behind her. She'd seen them when she cut through the parking lot of the supermarket five minutes ago.

She hadn't liked the look of them then and she sure didn't like the look of them now that they were following her.

One of them was white, one black, both in their mid-twenties. And they were thin - heroin thin with scruffy beards. They each had old flannel jackets that had seen better days and dark skullcaps.

And although she hadn't gotten too close, the wind had shifted letting her know that one, or probably both of them, were in desperate need of a bath.

Another wind blew against her now. Lou pulled up the collar of her jean jacket, although it didn't help much. She hitched her backpack up on her shoulder. She'd stayed late at her shift at the diner - not that she'd made much extra. People weren't really in a tipping mood these days.

And now these guys are going to take what little I did make, she thought. Anger and resentment ran through her right next to the fear.

She debated what to do. Cutting through the park would be faster and the park would probably be pretty empty with a storm kicking up and it getting close to dark.

She pictured the dark trees and winding paths. The city hadn't been keeping up the park and as a result, the trees and bushes were wildly overgrown creating lots of hiding spots.

A shiver ran through her. *But anyone I run into in there will not be someone I want to chat with.*

She glanced behind - the two men were a little farther back. If she turned the corner quick enough, they might not notice her heading to the park. If she stayed on the streets, though, it would easily take an extra fifteen minutes to get home.

Another wind, stronger this time, blew against her. The chill sliced right through to her bones.

Decision made. Lou picked up the pace, darted around the corner, and leaped over the chain link fence into the park. If she was lucky, they wouldn't realize what she'd done until-

The rattle of the chain link behind her told her she was not lucky tonight. *Shit.*

Moving faster, Lou headed deeper into the park. *Stupid. So stupid. I should have stayed on the road.*

Of course, there wouldn't have been much help there, either. People in this neighborhood didn't exactly leap to one another's defense.

A scuffle sounded behind her. Lou turned her head. They were closer. Two arms wrapped around her biceps as she collided into someone.

Her head whipped around. "Sorry," she said stepping back.

The two hands held her in place. "Hey beautiful. You can run into me any time."

The man was the Latino version of the other two. Except instead of a flannel jacket, he had on an old dark sweatshirt with the hood up.

Lou's voice turned hard. "Let me go."

"Not yet sweetheart. My friends and I were going to have a little party." He looked up. "Hey guys."

Lou looked behind her. The two guys she'd seen on the street. They'd actually been heading to the park. If she'd stayed on the damned street, she would have been fine.

Fear raced through her. "Get your hands off of me."

He shook her and her head jolted with action. Her backpack slipped down onto her elbow. He yanked it off her and tossed it at one of his friends. "See if there's anything good."

"Let me go," Lou said again, her voice shaking.

"Not until we're done." He smirked, taking a step back while keeping her in his grip. He looked her over. "You're a tiny little thing, aren't you? But that's good. I like tiny. Makes me feel big. Real big."

He pushed her toward the woods. "Come on."

Lou dug in her heels. "I'm not going anywhere with you."

Anger began to replace her fear. At that moment, she was sick of always being scared. Scared at school. Scared at home. Scared just living. And for whatever stupid reason, even though part of her mind yelled at her to just do what he said, she was done with being scared.

And somewhere deep inside of her Lou felt a binding snap loose.

The man holding her reared back with one hand, bringing it toward her face. With a speed that astonished her, Lou reached up and blocked it. Grabbing onto to the man's wrist she twisted it to a ninety-degree angle.

He screeched, dropping to his knees. "Let go bitch."

One of the other men ran at her. Keeping hold of the first guy's wrist she turned and kicked the other guy in the chest.

A crack sounded. He screamed and fell back, holding his side.

Lou's eyes went wide. *Were those his ribs?*

The third guy pulled a switchblade from his pocket, flipping it open.

Lou yanked on the guy she was holding, placing him between her and his knife-wielding friend.

"Tell your friend to get out of here or I'll break your wrist." She twisted his wrist for emphasis.

He yelled. "Get out of here, man."

His friend didn't seem interested in listening. He circled around her and tried to run at her.

Lou was faster.

She twirled her prisoner in between them again and shoved him, turning his wrist - hard. The bone snapped.

He screeched and fell to the ground. The man with the knife tripped over him with a yelp and fell onto his stomach.

The first man scrambled to his feet, cradling his wrist. He backed away from her. "You bitch. You broke my wrist."

The man Lou kicked also got to his feet holding his side. "Get up, Mike." He kicked Mike who was still lying face down. Mike didn't move.

Lou's eyes travelled from the man's ratty sneakers up to his skullcap. Nothing moved. A dark liquid began to seep from under him onto the path.

Lou took a step back in horror.

"You killed him." The Latino guy stared at her with accusing eyes.

Lou stumbled back from them. "I didn't mean- I didn't -" She looked up into the two men's eyes. Anger burned bright in them and a small dash of fear.

Lou slammed her mouth shut, turned on her heel, and ran.

CHAPTER 2

Henry Chandler walked across the sprawling lawn of his three hundred acre estate. His estate, which dated back to the late 1800s doubled as the business headquarters for his analytical firm, the Chandler Group. While most of the estate was lavish, his own home was a small cottage located just beyond the main building.

He'd walked the path from his office to his home more times than he could remember. But today an uncommon feeling joined him: stress - because in a short while he would introduce his unofficial son to his long 'dead' mother. He couldn't remember the last time he'd been this nervous.

He glanced at the tall, dark haired woman next to him. Her dark almond shaped brown eyes met his and his heart gave a little stutter.

"He'll understand, right?" he asked.

Jennifer Witt slipped her hand into his. "It's going to be fine."

He looked down at her. Henry stood at seven foot two and normally towered over people - especially women. Jen, however, was only fourteen inches shorter than him. One night when they went to dinner she'd worn heels and shortened the height differential to less than a foot.

"I know," he said.

She squeezed his hand. "But you're worrying anyway. I thought you Fortune 500 tycoons were known for your steely resolve."

"That's for work. In which case, I'm fearless."

Which was true. Henry had started the Chandler Group when he was just twenty-two, right out of college. His mother had 'died' four years earlier and he knew he needed to make a life for himself.

Actually, that wasn't entirely true. He could have just lived off his family's money and not done a thing with his life.

But he wanted something for himself - something he created. As a result, the Chandler Group, a world-renowned international think tank was born. Now almost twenty years later, he was sought after by heads-of-state for his analytical skills as well as the wealth of experts under his leadership.

But the meeting tonight eclipsed all the others in its importance.

"Is he home yet?" Jen asked.

Henry nodded as they cut through the blue spruces that surrounded his and Danny's home. The simple two-story cottage came into view. Lights shone through each window. Henry smiled. While he might second-guess a lot of his decisions regarding Danny, choosing to live in a simple home over a giant mansion was definitely one of his best.

The sun disappeared behind the horizon as Jen and Henry covered the short distance to the front door and opened it.

Danny Wartowski walked out of the kitchen. "So what's this big surprise?"

Henry looked at the boy he had unofficially adopted seven years ago. Danny was now five foot eight and seemed to get taller every week. His hair had darkened although it was not yet as dark as Henry's. But he still had those freckles and big brown eyes that made him look younger than his age.

Of course, he also had an off the charts IQ that made him seem much older than his chronological age as well.

Legally, Danny was an emancipated minor. But Henry and

Danny had easily fallen into the family routine. They had both needed that stability in their lives. They still did.

Henry looked at Jen who arched an eyebrow back at him. He turned back to Danny. "Um, how about you help me get dinner ready and then I'll tell you about it?"

Danny paused, watching Henry. "Okay," he said slowly.

Henry headed down the hall toward him, throwing an arm around Danny's shoulders, and leading him to the kitchen. "Come on. It will be fun."

An hour later, dinner was ready, the table was set, and Henry felt like he was about to have a heart attack.

Danny placed a water pitcher on the table while Jen walked over to Henry. "It's going to be okay," she said quietly.

The doorbell rang.

Henry's heart began to gallop. He turned to Danny. "There's someone here to see you."

"Who?" Danny asked.

Henry struggled for the right words. "Um, just, uh -"

Jen took pity on him. "Why don't I get the door and you can make the introductions?" She moved down the hall. Henry and Danny followed in her wake.

Jen glanced over her shoulder at Henry when she reached the door. Henry nodded back at her. Jen pulled the door open.

Standing on the front steps was a woman with a full head of white hair, cut into a sleek bob. She stepped in and the light from the hallway shone for a moment against her striking violet eyes - eyes the same color as Henry's.

Victoria Chandler smiled at everyone. "Good evening."

Henry stepped forward. "Danny, I'd like to introduce you to-"

Danny cut him off. "Your Mom." Danny walked forward and hugged her.

Victoria's shocked eyes found Henry's over Danny's shoulder. Henry looked back at her dumbfounded.

Jen laughed. "Serves you two right for trying to keep anything from him." She grinned at Danny. "How long have you known?"

Danny stepped back from Victoria, his grin a little sheepish. "Well, I've suspected since Henry told me about the bridge accident. But I was sure when Henry was abducted."

Henry shook his head. "Why didn't you tell me?"

Danny shrugged. "I figured you'd tell me when you were ready. And I'm guessing Victoria-"

"Grandma," Victoria cut in.

Danny smiled. "Right, Grandma had a reason for staying hidden. So can we eat now?"

Henry nodded. "Uh sure."

"Great." Danny offered his arm to Victoria. She took it with a smile.

Henry watched them walk down the hall together, knowing his mouth was gaping. "Who was that boy?"

Jen laughed. "I have no idea. Isn't he the shy, introverted one?"

"I guess not with family." He offered Jen his arm. "Shall we?"

She placed her hand on his. "Let's."

They walked toward the kitchen, hearing Victoria and Danny chatting away. Henry shook his head. This is not how he had pictured tonight going. He expected long explanations, maybe a little anger. But pure acceptance? He had not considered that possibility.

An hour later, Henry sat at the table and looked around in surprise and gratitude. This is what he had always wanted - a family. The only two missing were his sister, Delaney McPhearson and his best friend, Jake Rogan. Henry had finally convinced the two of them to take some time for themselves.

Feeling content, Henry pushed his coffee cup and dessert plate away. For the first time in a long while, he felt relaxed. He realized with a shock that he was finally having his Rockwell moment. The brick fireplace on the right hand side of the kitchen gave a warm glow to the room. Everyone was smiling and chatting. And even Moxy, Danny's shepherd mix, was curled up next to the fire.

He smiled across the table at Jen and she smiled back. *Yeah. This is good.*

A beeping sounded over by Danny and he pulled out his phone. Danny's face fell and he looked up at Henry.

Dread began to seep into Henry. "What's wrong?"

"I think I found one," Danny said.

"One what?" Victoria asked looking between the two of them.

Danny glanced at her before his gaze returned to Henry. "A Fallen."

CHAPTER 3

JEN WATCHED from the front door as Henry walked his mother to the helipad. After Henry saw his mother off, he was going to stop by the office and call Maddox Datson to see if he'd be willing to run down the Fallen. As far as Danny could tell, the girl was a teenager.

She probably doesn't even know what's happening to her, Jen thought. *Or what's going to happen to her.*

And Jen would know. Jen was a nephilim, the child of an angel and human, just like Henry. They were one type of angel that existed in this world. The other type they called Fallen: the full reincarnation of a Fallen angel.

Although I suppose there's actually three types, Jen thought thinking of Laney. *But Laney's the only one of her kind.*

A few months ago Laney, Henry, and Jake had learned that a group of Fallen was trying to round up teenagers who were just coming into their abilities or who might come into abilities. But the other group's goals for the kids weren't exactly heart warming. In fact, they were nightmare inducing.

Maddox had worked at the camps for years, trying to get kids out from the inside before he'd nearly lost his life. Jen, Henry,

Laney, Jake and a bunch of others had already found and liberated kids from two camps.

But the leads had dried up. This was the first clue they had to another young potential Fallen in weeks. Jen shook her head, hoping they'd get to this girl in time.

Jen watched Henry and Victoria until the tall evergreens that hid Henry's cottage from the main headquarters blocked them from view. It was weird. Henry and his mom were so close even though Victoria had basically been in hiding since Henry was eighteen.

And Victoria was the keeper of more secrets than any of them could probably imagine. She hadn't even told Henry about his own nature, letting him wonder for years why he had the abilities he did.

But even with all of that, you could feel the love between mother and son. That's what made the difference. Victoria might be secretive, but she was never secretive about how important Henry was to her - and Laney too.

Jen closed the door and turned around. Danny stood just a few feet away.

Jen smiled. "Hey. I didn't hear you there."

Danny nodded toward the door. "She's kind of cool, right?"

Victoria who lived in the world of information, who knew things about the Fallen that none of them could even begin to guess at, who had somehow even brought someone back to life, and who'd been married to one of the most powerful angels ever.

Jen smiled. "Cool is definitely the word. Now how about you help me clean up the dishes?"

"Okay." Danny followed Jen into the kitchen. They worked in a comfortable silence. Jen tackled the sink. Danny took the table. Moxy once again curled up in her dog bed in front of the fireplace.

Jen was finishing up the last few dishes when Danny, who was wiping down the table, spoke. "Jen? Can I ask you a question?"

Jen stopped loading the dishwasher and looked at him over her shoulder. "I suppose."

"Um, it's about your parents."

Jen turned around to look at him, surprise filtering through her. "Um, okay. Shoot."

Danny gestured to the table.

Jen wiped her hands off on a towel, walked over to him, and sat down. "Go ahead."

Danny looked at her and then away. He traced an imaginary pattern on the table. "I was just wondering, who'd you get your powers from - your Mom or your Dad?"

Jen sat back, an image of her mom floating through her mind - dark hair and eyes like Jen's. "I don't know. I never met my Dad and my Mom disappeared when I was seven. I can't remember seeing her with any special skills. It could have been either of them."

"And you got your abilities early, right?"

"I was nine." Jen paused. "I think your abilities show up when you need them."

Danny met her eyes, understanding from another child of abuse. "And you needed them young."

"And I needed them young," Jen agreed simply.

Of course, none of it was that simple. She still remembered letting herself into the apartment that she had shared with her mother. She'd been in the second grade. She'd been wearing her favorite pink dress and her mom had braided her hair that morning - just like every morning.

But as soon as Jen had stepped back in the door that afternoon, she had felt the emptiness. She'd searched the apartment and nothing was missing - nothing except her Mom. And she'd known, deep down, that her mom was gone.

Jen had managed a week on her own. She got herself to school, although she hadn't been able to manage the braids. She ate what little was left in the kitchen. A neighbor finally realized what had happened and turned her in.

Jen spent the next two years in six foster homes - each home progressively worse than the last. In that last home, when she was nine, her abilities had kicked in.

Two of her foster brothers had tormented her unendingly, hitting her and locking her away when they could get away with it - which was often. The day her abilities had kicked in she had climbed the tall oak tree in the yard - hoping she could avoid them.

She hadn't - they followed her up.

She still remembered how scared she was. One of them grabbed her. Before she could even scream, he tossed her out of the tree. Her abilities were the only reason she survived. She'd run away two days later - after hospitalizing both boys.

She shook her head. *No need to focus on that.*

"You know, my family wasn't always very nice to me," Danny said.

Jen looked at him quietly, surprised yet again. Danny never talked about his past. She knew he was born somewhere in the Appalachia's, in a town that grew up around coal mining. A sensitive smart kid like Danny would not have had an easy time of it.

"Do you know I have three brothers?" Danny asked.

Jen shook her head. "No. I didn't know that."

Danny nodded, not meeting her eyes. "Yeah. I'm the youngest. My mom, she died when I was I five. But I remember she used to sing me to sleep. Frank Sinatra - 'I've Got You Under My Skin'."

Jen smiled, trying to remember her mother doing something that sweet. She couldn't.

Danny let out a breath and Jen stayed silent. He obviously needed to talk.

"My Dad - he thought I should be tougher - that I shouldn't waste so much time on books. I read one of Henry's articles when I was eight and wrote him. He wrote me back. A few months later he came to visit. Talked to my father about sending me to college. My father didn't want me to go, of course. He wanted me to toughen up, be a man. And what good was college going to do for a coal miner?"

Danny took a breath. "Somehow Henry convinced him. But

college, it wasn't for me. I was terrified of going back home. Then Henry offered me a place here. At first, he even got a governess."

Danny rolled his eyes. "I think he was watching the 'Sound of Music' right before he came up with the idea. But soon, it was just kind of me and Henry. Once I started working for Chandler HQ, I checked up on my family. Just to see."

"And?" Jen prompted gently.

"And they get weekly deposits of 5,000 dollars."

Jen felt her mouth fall open before she recovered herself. "Danny, you know Henry-"

He waved away her words. "Trust me. I understand. It was the only way they would let me go. I'm okay with it. I'm grateful, in fact. But the reason I'm telling you this, is that Henry *is* my family."

Jen nodded, thinking of the Witt family who had adopted her when she was eleven, after she'd been on the streets for two years. They had taken her in and given her love. Blood didn't always determine family. "I know."

Danny took a breath and looked at her. "So I need you be careful with him, okay?"

And the surprises kept coming. Although being she spent so much time with Henry and Danny, she should have expected Danny to notice. Touched, Jen reached out and grasped his hand. "I'll be careful. I promise."

CHAPTER 4

DEWITT, NY

MADDOX SAT at the edge of the playground watching five-year-old Max Simmons play in a sandbox. A couple of other older kids ran around playing tag. Two more were on the swings.

None of them paid any attention to the little brown haired boy. But Max didn't seem to mind.

The park was busy. Parents were scattered around the playground chatting, but none made eye contact with Maddox or looked in his direction.

Maddox once again scanned the area looking for any threats. He didn't find any and didn't expect to. Laney had asked him to keep an eye on Kati and Max until she got back and figured out how to keep them safe. So far, he'd been with them for three months.

He had no problem with that. Laney had saved his life and taken out the bastard who'd made his life miserable for the last ten years. He'd do anything she asked.

He owed her. Big.

Besides, he thought as he watched Kati Simmons walk down

the path toward him, there was something really nice about living a normal life after what he'd been through. He went food shopping, had seen a few kids movies, and he'd even been to the beach. He shook his head. And perhaps most surprising, he'd enjoyed almost all of it.

Kati stepped next to him, handing him a cup of coffee. "You know, you're scaring away everyone who looks at you."

Maddox looked down at Kati. At six foot six, he was a full foot taller than her. She and Max shared their brown hair but where Max's eyes were blue, Kati's were brown. "What?"

Kati gave a little laugh. "You - long dark hair, black leather jacket, scowling at everyone in the park. I'm surprised no one's called the cops on you."

Maddox shrugged. "Actually, I think one lady was going to until Max came over and gave me a hug."

"So, you're saying my five-year-old saved you from being hassled by the cops?"

A grin reluctantly tugged across his face. "Guess so."

Kati's eyes drifted to Max. He'd moved onto the slide. "How's he doing?"

"Good. He's played mainly by himself or at least, with his imaginary friends."

At her look of alarm, Maddox put up his hands. "All the other kids are older. It's not a big deal and he seems pretty content. He's only looked over here a few times since we got here. No more than any other kid looked to their parents."

Kati let out a breath. "Good. That's good."

"He's okay, Kati. No ill effects."

"I know. I just -" She sighed, her gaze falling on Max again. "I just want him safe."

Maddox nodded. Kati and Max had been caught in the crossfire down in Pennsylvania a few months ago. Kati had then been caught again a short time later and had come very close to losing her life.

Kati worried the brush with violence was going to negatively affect Max. But as far as Maddox could see, there hadn't been any real side effect. It was dark when everything had happened and Max was really too young to understand.

Although Max had developed an awful lot of imaginary friends since then. But what did Maddox know? He hadn't exactly spent much time around little kids. Maybe that was normal.

But Kati was a different story. Maddox had only met her after everything, but he could tell she was terrified. But Kati wasn't scared for herself. Her fear was all for her son.

Maddox knew Kati was having trouble not surrounding Max with bubble wrap and locking him away. He tried to hide his smile. Instead, with Laney's help, she'd given him a six foot six nephilim as a bodyguard.

Maddox's phone rang. He glanced down before answering. "Hey Henry."

"Hey Maddox. How are Kati and Max doing?"

Kati indicated she was going to push Max on the swings.

Maddox nodded watching her walk away. He leaned back against the tree behind him. "Good. How are you?"

"Good, but I have a request to make of you."

Maddox groaned. "Let me guess. Clark got in touch with you."

Clark was Agent Matthew Clark of the Special Investigative Agency (SIA) an offshoot of the Department of Defense. He'd been hounding Maddox for months to join. While Maddox liked the idea of tracking down renegade Fallen, he wasn't ready to leave his present assignment. If he was being honest, he wasn't sure he'd ever be ready to leave it.

"Uh no. At least not this week," Henry said. "But I have a case I was hoping you could look into. It could be a Fallen."

Maddox watched a man in a blue fleece walk into the playground area, his gaze searching the children. Maddox straightened up from the tree. The man broke into a grin as a pair of boys rushed over to him.

Maddox relaxed again. "Henry, it's not that I don't want to help. I won't leave Kati and Max unprotected. And Laney and

Jake are on a vacation. I really don't want to call them back from it."

Henry sighed. "I don't either."

"Is there anyone else you could send?"

Henry's voice was thoughtful. "Actually, I think there might be."

CHAPTER 5

DETROIT, MICHIGAN

JEN WALKED up the cement steps of the Fourteenth Precinct of the Detroit Police Department. Detroit had the honor of having four of the most dangerous neighborhoods in the United States. And the attack that had alerted Danny occurred smack dab in the middle of one of them.

Jen pushed open the double doors. The stench hit her immediately - a combination of body odor and urine. She wrinkled her nose. *Lovely.*

The decor didn't do much to detract from the smell. Pale green walls as far as the eye could see and a tile floor that had been all the rage in 1965.

It was a Sunday just after noon and the lobby was pretty quiet. One cop helped an old woman toward the back. She was in her nightgown and slippers. An anxious man and woman sat waiting in chairs that Jen wouldn't touch without a Hazmat suit.

Jen knew that cops weren't actually much of a deterrent to crime, but if this was what the lobby of the station looked like, she was pretty sure she had no interest in seeing the holding cells. And she couldn't imagine anyone else would either.

Jen walked up to the sergeant behind the big wooden desk. His attention was directed at the newspaper in front of him.

She stopped, waiting for the man to look at her. A few seconds passed and then a few more. She cleared her throat. "Excuse me."

The man put up a single finger. "Hold on a sec." He finished reading his article while Jen imagined yanking him from his chair by the collar.

Finally he looked up. "What can I-?" His words abruptly ended as he took his first look at Jen. His eyes widened. He sat up straighter in his chair and ran a hand through his thinning hair.

Oh buddy, you have no chance, she thought.

Jen was used to that reaction, although she never really understood it. When she looked in the mirror all she saw was a woman who obviously had one Korean parent and one Caucasian. She wasn't really sure what everyone else saw.

Out loud, she said, "I'm looking for Detective Cazini."

"And who may I say is looking for her?"

Jen reached into her jacket pocket and pulled out her shiny new badge. "Agent Witt."

It was the first time she'd used her badge. SIA Agent Clark had deputized her, Henry, Jake, Maddox, and Laney a few months ago - right after they had successfully taken down Samyaza, the fallen angel who once again had seemed hell bent on ruling mankind.

Jen still wasn't sure what she thought about the 'honor' of being a member of the SIA. But right now, credentials would help her along.

"She's upstairs. Second floor, homicide." The sergeant went to step off his chair. "Why don't I show-"

Jen cut him off and headed toward the entrance of the bullpen. "I'm sure I'll find it."

Jen didn't miss the crestfallen look on the man's face as he buzzed her through.

Jen strode down the hall, ignoring the occasional curious glance. Spying the stairs, she took them two at a time. She made a right at the second floor landing.

Third door on the left, the letters o-m-i-c-i-d-e were on the door. The outline of the H was barely visible. Apparently, it had been missing for a while.

There were only two occupants in the room and one was a man with a broom. She turned toward the female. "Detective Cazini?"

Cazini turned around. She was easily pushing fifty, which seemed odd for a detective. She should have climbed the ranks by now if she was in it for the long haul. Most cops Jen knew did their twenty or twenty-five and then were on to their new career.

"Yeah?" Cazini said. She had the voice and skin of a lifetime smoker.

Jen flashed her badge. "Agent Witt. I wanted to ask you about a case you caught."

Cazini blew out a breath. "Just make it quick."

Jen pulled over a chair. "The stabbing in Maxwell Park last night. In your report, it states that a young girl was assaulted by three assailants and got away."

"Yeah. One guy - looks like he fell on his knife during the fight. The other two: a couple of busted ribs and a broken wrist. They say some little teenager did that to all of them."

"You don't believe them?"

The detective shrugged. "Each of them has a rap sheet a couple of pages long, mostly drug related. I figure they were probably high at the time."

"But their tox screens came back clean."

"Well, maybe some sort of hallucination."

Jen tried to keep her anger in check. *A shared hallucination that resulted in actual injuries?* She thought of her friend Rocky Martinez and the kind of cop she was. A stab of grief rolled through her. This detective couldn't hold a candle to Rocky.

Jen's anger at Rocky's death added an edge to her voice. "Did you at least get a description of the girl?"

"They said she was small with dark hair, light eyes."

"Did you make any effort to find her?"

Cazini laughed. "Right - on the word of two druggies. I don't think so."

Jen stood. "Well thanks Detective. You've been almost helpful."

Cazini narrowed her eyes. "What did you say?"

"Pretty sure you heard me. You have a young girl who was attacked by three assailants and you've made no effort to find her. Sloppy is too clean a word for your work. Have a nice night."

Jen turned her back on the detective leaving her spluttering. She pushed the woman from her mind. It looked like finding this girl was going to be a bit more complicated. And she prayed she was the only one looking.

CHAPTER 6

Jen walked down the path in the park that led to the crime scene. Trees towered above her and blocked out what little light the grey sky provided. The attack on the girl occurred at night, making the park much darker than it was now.

Jen glanced up at the row of light poles that lined the path. She doubted any of them worked. And due to Detroit's economic woes, she didn't think lighting them was going to be a priority any time soon.

Jen imagined the place at night with a storm moving in and shuddered. *Gutsy kid walking through here.*

She checked her phone. *Should only be another couple of feet.* One of the beat cops who had uncovered the body had actually put the map coordinates from his phone on the report.

Even in the dim light, she could see the discoloration from where the blood had seeped into the grey top. She knelt down, looking around. That night this spot was dark, secluded, and cold. *That poor kid.*

Detective Cazini wrote in her report that she had canvassed the area and not found anything. But being Jen had seen the detective live and in person, she had no faith in that report.

Jen looked around, wishing she had gotten here earlier. Well she'd just have to make do.

To be honest, though, she wasn't even sure what she was looking for. She wasn't a cop, no matter what the badge in her jacket suggested.

Even with training, any training, she didn't think it would be easy to distinguish between something the kid had left behind and something someone else had dropped. To put it kindly, the park was not well maintained - trash littered the place.

Jen walked back to the blood spot, trying to picture the attack in her head. She ignored the ramblings from the guys about trying to help the girl and focused on what they said. The girl had kicked one of guys in the ribs and used the other as a shield.

Jen pulled out her flashlight and illuminated the bushes and trees that ran along the path. Her hopes dimmed. Cazini was right. There wasn't anything here - nothing of use at least.

Her light landed on a bench a few feet away. Jen squinted. There was something there. Something dark.

Jen walked over to the bench and squatted down, pulling out her gloves. She wasn't doing it to preserve any evidence, but to avoid whatever grossness currently inhabited the space.

Pushing some newspapers out of the way, she saw a red backpack and pulled it out. A few books had fallen out. Jen gathered them as well.

The book on the top of the pile was *A Separate Peace* by John Knowles. Jen smiled. She remembered having to read that in high school, although for the life of her she couldn't remember the plot.

She tucked the books into the backpack and pulled the notebook out, flipping through it. Notes on the French Revolution were written in a neat handwriting. Jen placed the notebook back in the bag and zipped it up.

Slinging the pack over her shoulder, she headed out of the park. *All right, let's see who you belong too.*

CHAPTER 7

Lou jogged down her street, her eyes peeled for any one walking up on her. Ever since the night in the park she'd been extra vigilant when she was out. She pictured the man who'd grabbed her and her heart began to beat faster. She heard the snap of his wrist again. *How did I do that?*

She'd looked up wrist bones to see if they were easy to break. They weren't supposed to be. But she'd read that some people had more fragile bones than others. Maybe that's why she'd broken it so easily and the same for the other guy's ribs.

And the truth was, it had been easy. No harder than wringing a towel or kicking a piece of paper. She pictured the fear in the men's eyes when they looked at her. What had that all been? How had she done it?

The streetlight above her came to life. Memories of her mother and grandmother warning her to be home before the streetlights came on flashed through her. Knives of grief stabbed through her making her catch her breath. There was no one to worry about her when the streetlights came on any more.

She picked up her pace anyway. She'd had to stay late at school to replace the books she'd lost in the park. The librarian had not been sympathetic.

Of course, she'd probably heard every excuse under the sun in her thirty years at the school library. Lou's assault story hadn't even made the woman blink. She'd merely held out her hand for the seventy-eight dollars to replace the books.

Biting her lip, Lou held back the tears. Seventy-eight dollars. She could not afford that.

In her head, she re-arranged the bills trying to make up for the loss. *Maybe if Charlotte takes an extra shift we can make up the difference.*

She turned the corner and came to a stop. Her sister Charlotte's car was in the drive.

No, Lou wailed internally. If Charlotte was home this early, it meant she'd been fired - again.

Lou shoved the feelings of being overwhelmed away. *I will not cry. I will not cry*, she chanted silently as she made her way up the rickety three steps to her porch.

Before going to the door, she walked over to the living room window. Peering in, she saw her sister and two male 'friends' passed out.

Lou stepped back, her shoulders dropping. Her chest welled, and she repeated her refrain - *I will not cry. I will not cry.*

Lou went to insert her key in the lock but the door was already ajar. Shaking her head at her sister's carelessness, she eased it open, tensing when it creaked.

No sound came from the living room. Carefully, she closed the door behind her. She ran up the stairs as quietly as she could, avoiding the squeaky stair tread four from the top.

Crossing the small landing at the top of the stairs to her room, she closed the door behind her and turned the lock. She leaned against the door, her heart hammering, and listened. No noise came from downstairs. She let out a breath. *Thank God.*

Pushing away from the door, Lou crossed the room to her closet. She reached around on the top shelf and felt the soft fur of her old stuffed turtle.

Pulling him down, she sat on her bed. Flipping him over, she carefully removed her stash of cash. Long ago, she'd learned that any money her sister found would quickly disappear. She counted out the bills - three hundred and twelve dollars.

Lou felt the weight settle against her chest. She leaned back against the headboard, pulling the turtle to her chest. It wasn't enough. They were already a couple of months behind in the rent. And they weren't going to make it this month either.

Lou's part time job at the diner didn't pay much. But even if she quit school, she didn't have much of a chance at a full time job - people with Masters degrees lined up at fast food joints for jobs right now.

And her sister had tossed her job away. Lou was sure of it. *Damn it.* Lou rubbed her eyes, denying the tears there the chance to fall.

"You'll figure something out. You always do," she said out loud. But the words didn't make her feel any more confident.

The doorbell rang.

Lou's head jerked up. *No, no, no.* She did not need Charlotte and her friends waking up right now. She needed to get her homework done and get something to eat before they woke up.

A second thought made her go still. *Oh God, what if it's a surprise inspection by Children's and Families? Do they know about the park?*

One glance in the living room had told her the whole story about how her sister had spent the day. The bowls were in plain sight as were the beer cans.

In her mind, Lou calculated how fast she could clean it all up. She shook her head, feeling despair run through her. There wasn't enough time to do that, get her sister awake, and clean house of her new friends.

Stuffing the turtle under her blanket, Lou unlocked her bedroom door and ran down the stairs. A strange buzz traveled over her skin. She yanked her hand from the bannister. *What the hell was that?*

The doorbell rang again. Lou glanced into the living room as she passed. Her sister stirred. *Stay asleep. Please stay asleep.*

Lou unlocked the door, but kept the chain on. A woman, part Asian in a suit stood outside the door. Oh God, it had to be a social worker. No one else dressed like that in this part of town.

The woman's confident demeanor though made her rethink her first impression. *Oh shit. A cop.*

Lou kept her expression neutral. "Can I help you?"

The woman smiled and Lou was taken aback. The woman was seriously pretty. "Hi. I'm looking for Louisa Thomas."

"Um, Lou. That's me."

The woman pulled a badge from her pocket. "Lou, I'm Agent Jen Witt. I wanted to speak with you about an incident in the park last night."

Lou felt her eyes widen before she could control herself. "What incident?"

Jen smiled. "Maybe we could talk inside." She held up a backpack. "Is this yours?"

Lou's heart pounded. If her books were in there, she could get some money back from the librarian. "Um yeah. Where'd you find it?"

"Two gentlemen who said they were attacked by a young woman in the park the other day say it belongs to her. Another man died in the attack."

Shock rooted Lou in place. *Died?* She pictured the man on the ground, the blood seeping out from him.

"Lou?"

Lou's gaze flew to the agent's face. She struggled to keep her face neutral. "Um, I don't know anything about that. But could I have my bag please?"

The agent paused before handing it over. "Sure. Now how about we chat for a few minutes?"

Lou took the pack, trying not to laugh with joy as she felt the weight. The books, at least most of them, were still in there. She dropped the bag next to her and looked behind her. "Um, my sister's not home right now. And she'd be real unhappy if I let someone in without permission."

Lou tried not to laugh out loud at the lie. *Charlotte upset about anything other than people stealing her weed? Right.*

"When will she be home?" Agent Witt asked.

Lou heard the sound of someone moving about in the other room. "Um, not sure. Why don't you try back tomorrow or the next day?" She slammed the door not waiting for the agent to reply.

Lou locked the door, intending to head right back upstairs.

Charlotte stumbled out of the living room, scratching her hair. "Who's that?" she slurred.

Lou looked at her sister and marveled at how much she'd changed. When she was younger, Lou had thought Charlotte was the most beautiful girl ever. She knew she'd never be as beautiful as her big sister.

Now that same sister stood in the hallway in underwear and a stained Mickey Mouse t-shirt. The dark curls Lou had once envied hung limp around her sister's face. Her sister probably hadn't showered in days. And dark circles under her blue eyes made her seem much older than her twenty years.

Lou pulled her backpack onto her shoulder. "Uh, no one. Just some lady selling magazines."

"What are you doing here? Don't you have school?"

"It's after five."

Charlotte gave Lou a blank look.

"School's over," Lou said.

"Oh. All right." Charlotte drifted back into the living room, all interest in her sister lost.

Lou tried not to feel hurt. But even with years of practice, she wasn't able to keep out the sting. She headed back up the stairs. Her sister's scream stopped her.

A man's voice whipped up the stairs. "Where is it, bitch? What did you do with my money?"

Running back down, Lou sprinted into the living room. One of the guys her sister had been partying with earlier had his hand wrapped around her throat.

Lou ran across the room, but the second man tackled her to the ground. She looked up at her sister. Charlotte's hands fumbled at the hands gripping her throat, cutting off her air.

Terror gripped Lou. *He's going to kill her.*

CHAPTER 8

Jen stood out on the front porch. She knew there were more people inside than just the girl. Before knocking, she'd glanced in the living room window and had seen the passed-out group.

There were three of them. She thought one might be Lou's sister Charlotte but she had no idea who the guys were. Jen didn't press the issue with Lou, though, because underneath all the girl's toughness, Jen could tell she was scared.

Walking down the porch steps, Jen stopped and looked back at the dilapidated house. She'd done some digging on Lou after finding out she'd been the one in the park. It hadn't been that hard to track her down.

Detective Cazini - if she had tried - could probably have found her just as quickly. Jen shook her head. Although it was probably better that Jen found her and not the detective. Lord knew what Cazini would have done.

Louisa and Charlotte Thomas had grown up in this house. Their Mom had been killed in a home invasion here five years ago. The girls and their grandmother had survived.

The grandmother had passed away two years ago of a heart attack also in this house. And by some miracle, Charlotte had gotten custody of Lou. But it had been a tenuous situation at best.

There were a number of threats to revoke custody, but they all seemed to fall through the cracks.

In fact, no one from Children's and Families had visited the Thomas household in over a year - even though the sister had been busted twice for possession.

The foster home Jen had lived in before running away had the same pall of despair and neglect over it. Even if this kid didn't have any abilities, Jen wasn't about to leave her here. There had to be a better situation for her somewhere.

Jen hadn't felt any connection when the girl had opened the door, but it didn't mean she wasn't the right one. It just meant she wasn't a nephilim. Jen could sense other nephilim. Fallen, however, could sense one another as well as nephilim and there was still a chance Lou was one of them.

Jen closed her eyes, straining to hear. She could just make out the murmur of voices behind the door and footsteps on the stairs. Enhanced hearing was a new ability she'd been honing lately.

A scream pierced the air.

Jen's eyes flew open and she vaulted up the steps. She glanced in the window next to the front door. A man held Lou's sister by the throat. Another man tackled Lou to the floor.

Jen tried the door but it was locked. She stepped back and blasted it with a front kick. The door flew off the hinges landing ten feet away.

Jen walked over the door and stood in the entrance of the living room. The men stared at her, their jaws slack.

"I'm going to have to ask you two to release those ladies," Jen said.

The one holding Charlotte flung the girl to the floor and sneered. "Let's see what you got, cop,"

Jen tried not to sigh. This is what she got when she wore a suit. Everyone thought she was a cop.

The asshole ran across the room. He threw a right punch.

Jen easily stepped out of the way, throwing an elbow at his jaw.

He screamed. Grabbing the back of his head, she kneed him in the face.

She was about to take him down when she realized the knee had done it for her. She dropped his unconscious body to the floor.

She turned to the guy holding Lou. "Let. Her. Go."

He did, taking a run at Jen.

God, these guys are stupid.

At the last second, Jen stepped aside, throwing out her right hand, clotheslining him. He crashed into it with such a force, that he actually flipped almost completely around before landing in a heap.

Jen glanced at both men. Out cold. She walked over to Lou and extended her hand.

Lou stared up at her with big eyes before she grasped Jen's hand and let Jen haul her up. As soon as Lou gained her feet, she ran to her sister.

"Is she okay?" Jen asked as she pulled out her cell.

Charlotte groaned in response. "I'm okay," she mumbled.

Lou looked back at Jen, fear on her face. "Who are you calling?"

Jen nudged her chin toward the two men on the floor. One had begun to moan. "The cops. For these two."

Lou jumped up and ran across the room incredibly fast.

Jen raised an eyebrow. Fallen fast.

Lou grabbed Jen's hand. "No. Please don't."

Jen looked into Lou's eyes, seeing herself years before. Jen knew if she called, Children and Families would be notified. If their track record was any indication, though, it might mean nothing. But it also could mean the girl would be moved. Although as Jen looked around the room, she realized that might not be a bad thing.

"Please," Lou said.

Jen closed the phone. "Okay. But we need to talk."

Lou nodded, looking from the door to the men on the floor. "Okay."

CHAPTER 9

FORTY-FIVE MINUTES LATER, Jen made her way to Lou's back door. She knocked softly and waited only a few seconds before the chains rattled and the door opened.

Her blue eyes wide and her face pale, Lou stepped back and ushered Jen in. "Agent Witt."

Jen stepped past her. "Call me Jen."

Lou stood shifting from foot to foot. "Um, Are they- Did you-?"

Jen took pity and answered the question Lou couldn't seem to form. "I dropped them off in an alley. No one saw me. No one should connect them back to you or your sister."

"Okay. Good."

Jen looked around. "Where *is* your sister?"

Taking a seat, Lou nodded toward the stairs. "Sleeping. I brought her up." Lou's brow furrowed.

Jen sat across from her. "What?"

"I carried her up the stairs. It was as if she weighed nothing. And then the other night in the park-." Lou darted a glance at Jen before clasping her mug tightly, her eyes focused on it.

"I know about the park," Jen said, softly. "You fought off those three guys."

"I didn't mean to hurt anyone. I was - They followed me. I was only trying to get away."

"I know that, too. But I'm guessing that's the first time you realized you had some skills?"

Lou looked at Jen. "The way you moved before. You're fast. Really fast."

Jen nodded. "Yes. I'm fast, strong, and I heal quickly when I'm hurt. And I think you're like me."

Lou looked at Jen for a moment and then shook her head. "I'm not like you."

"Yeah, you are. I've seen enough to know that."

Lou's face was pale. "You can't know that."

Jen paused. "When I came to the door, did you have any physical reaction to me?"

Lou leaned back a little in her chair, speaking slowly. "Not when I opened the door, but before. It was almost like an electric current ran through me. Why? Did you feel it?"

"No. But it does confirm some things for me." Jen stopped talking, trying to figure out the best way to break Lou's nature to her. She thought back to when she'd learned what she could do. How scared she felt, how alone, but also how powerful.

She looked at Lou. The kid was tough. And from what Jen could tell, she'd probably been taking care of Charlotte rather than the other way round for the last two years. She could handle it. She might even welcome it.

Jen met Lou's eyes. "First, let me tell you that there are other people out there like you - with skills like you."

"What? I've never heard of them."

"Well, most keep a low profile." Jen's eyes strayed to the schoolbooks on the countertop. Her eyes fell on the world history book and she remembered the names of Fallen from the past that a Chandler scientist had uncovered. "Did you study the Bolshevik Revolution?"

Lou nodded, giving Jen a curious look. "Yeah. It was a popular movement that toppled the Romanov dynasty."

"Did you learn anything about Rasputin?"

"Yeah. I did a paper on him. He was -." Lou's eyes went wide. "I'm like him?"

"Sort of. I think his nickname the mad monk was pretty accurate. But do you remember how he died?"

"He was poisoned, shot, beaten, stabbed, and finally drowned."

Jen nodded. "Each time they tried to kill him, they failed. A mortal man would have died from any of those attacks. He didn't."

Lou's eyes were wide. "When he was pulled from the river, one of his arms had worked its way free of its bindings. They say he was alive when he went in."

Jen nodded. "I bet he would have lived if the river hadn't been covered in ice. Like I said, we heal quickly. We're not easy to kill."

Lou stared at Jen, her mouth open. Jen let her have a moment to let everything sink in - at least as much as it could.

Finally, Lou seemed to pull herself together. "So what are we? Are we lab rats?"

Jen studied the girl. Smudges were under her pale blue eyes. Her dark hair was a wild halo around her head. The kid had not had an easy life. And Jen was pretty sure this news was not going to make it easier.

But there was no keeping the truth from her. Jen sighed. "What do you know about angels?"

"Angels?" Lou's eyebrows shot up so fast, Jen worried they'd never return to their normal position.

Jen blew out a breath. This was not going well. She spied a knife on the counter, an idea forming. Rolling up her sleeves, she walked over to the sink and pulled her own knife from the sheath on her belt.

Lou leaped up. "Wh-what are you doing?"

Jen gripped the knife. "It's okay. I'm just going to give you a little demonstration."

Jen grimaced as she slid the knife blade across her forearm. She held her arm over the sink as the blood dripped down the sides.

"Are you crazy?" Lou shrieked. She backed away toward the door.

Jen rinsed the knife off. "No. Not crazy. Just different."

Jen grabbed some paper towel from the holder next to the sink and soaked them. Jen wiped the blood away. She held her arm out for Lou to see.

The cut began to fuse together. Another few seconds and all that was left was an angry red mark lining her forearm. Then slowly the red turned pink, before disappearing.

Lou stood still, her mouth gaping open. "How- what- who are you?"

CHAPTER 10

Jen stood leaning against the counter calmly rolling down her sleeves. Lou felt like she'd just entered the Twilight Zone. How the hell had Jen just done that?

Lou made her way back to the table, slumping into her chair, her legs feeling weak. "That was - you think I'm like you? Because I'm not. When I get hurt, I bleed and it doesn't heal like that."

Jen shrugged. "Everyone comes into their abilities at different times. I'm guessing yours were activated the other night in the park.

"Activated? What, like a robot?"

Jen smiled. "No. Not a robot. You're an angel."

Lou stared at her. What the hell was this woman talking about? She shook her head, thinking she would have believed her more if she had actually said robot. Religion didn't play much of a role around here, not since her grandma died.

"Yeah." Lou drew out the word. "See, I'm not really the church going type. So, I don't think-"

"You don't have to be religious." Jen tilted her head to the side. "In fact, they come in pretty much all shapes and sizes, all ethnicities and religions. Or lack thereof."

"So, you're one?"

"I'm a nephilim, the offspring of a fallen angel and a human."

"So your mom was an angel?"

Jen shrugged. "Honestly, I don't know if it was my mom or my dad."

Lou inspected Jen. Her demeanor was cool, even standoffish. And Lou realized it wasn't because she was a cop. It was because she was on her own - or at least had been - just like Lou.

Another thought struck her. Her eyes flew to Jen. "Am I going to grow wings?"

Jen laughed. "No. Wings are not part of the package."

"So you can't fly?"

"Not unless I'm in a plane."

Lou stared at her trying to think of something to say. "Do all nephilim have powers?" Lou asked slowly.

Jen shook her head. "No. From what I understand, very few do."

"So I'm also a nephilim?" Lou asked trying to figure out which of her parents could have had powers. It was ridiculous. Her father had died of lung cancer when she was three. And her mom had been killed. If either of them had powers, they hadn't done them any good.

Jen paused. "Actually, no. You're the other type of superhuman. You're what we call a Fallen."

"A Fallen?" A vague memory fluttered through Lou's mind - her Grandma talking to her about evil entering the world through the fallen angels. "Wait you don't mean fallen angels, do you?"

Jen nodded.

Lou scrambled to form thoughts through her confusion. "But, they fell, assuming it ever actually happened, forever ago. And I was born fifteen years ago. So I can't be one."

"I know. It sounds incredible. The Fallen are reborn time and time again and live out their lives with their powers."

Lou paused trying to take it all in and failing. "Wait - you said you're the child of an angel and a human. Does that mean if I have kids, my kids will have powers?"

"It's possible," Jen said.

Lou stared at this strange woman in her kitchen. What the hell was going on? She remembered the angel picture her Grandma had kept in her bedroom. Her Grandma said the angels would look after them.

Lou had moved the picture into her own bedroom after her Grandmother had died. But she didn't really believe they existed, did she? I mean, an objective look at her life made it pretty clear there was no one besides Lou looking out for Lou.

Lou shook her head. Okay, she didn't know what the deal was with that whole cutting trick but obviously this woman was a few eggs short of a dozen. Why was she even listening to her?

Lou stood up. "Look, I appreciate you helping me and Charlotte out but I think it's time for you to go. I don't know what brand of crazy you're trying to sell here but I'm not buying."

Jen stayed where she was. The silence grew between them.

Lou struggled to figure out what to do. The woman was crazy but she was also pretty strong. There was no chance Lou would be able to get her out of the house on her own. And if she called the cops-

Lou sighed. *Damn.*

"I know it's a bit much to take in all at once," Jen said. "Unlike you, I had years to get used to the fact that I had abilities before I learned why I had them."

Lou let the exasperation she was feeling into her words. "Look, I don't have any special abilities. I don't know what that was in the park, but it was probably just adrenaline or something. So I'm going to have to ask you to leave."

Jen nodded and stood, pulling a business card from her pocket. "Here's my number. If you need to talk to me, or if you need help, give me a call. I'm going to stay in town for another few days."

Lou pocketed the card. "Yeah sure, whatever." She looked at Jen for a minute. "If I have these abilities, which I don't, why do you care?"

Jen went silent.

Lou could tell she was debating whether or not to tell her the truth. Lou tensed, waiting for the lie.

"Sometimes, when a certain group learns about a person with abilities, they try to recruit them."

"So what? You try to beat them to the punch?"

Jen shook her head. "No. I'm not trying to recruit you into anything."

"So why are you here?"

"This other group has been known to kill to get people into their group."

"What? Like hurt me?"

Jen paused, her eyes staring into Lou's.

Lou forced herself to meet the woman's gaze.

"No," Jen said softly. "They go after the recruit's family. They get rid of the people close to them. Leave the recruit vulnerable and alone."

Lou felt cold. "Are you threatening my sister?"

Jen let out a sigh. "I'm explaining this really badly. Basically, I think you and your sister might be in danger. And I want to help if I can."

Lou stood up, walked to the back door, and held it open. "Thanks, but we don't need any help."

Jen hesitated for a moment before she stood and walked to the door. She stopped next to Lou, looking down at her. "I hope you're right. But if anything feels off, call me, okay?"

"Yeah, sure. And thanks for helping before." Lou didn't meet her eyes. She just wished the strange woman would go.

Jen walked out and Lou let out a breath. She watched Jen walk down the porch steps and around the side of the house before shutting the door. She bolted the lock and leaned against the door. The woman was crazy - that's all there was too it.

But a small voice niggled at her from the corner of her mind. *But what if she isn't?*

CHAPTER 11

Lou walked down the hallway of Martin Luther King High School. Built in 1970, it hadn't been renovated in years. Parts of the second floor were completely blocked off for fear someone would crash through. The chalkboards were too cracked to write on, forcing the more concerned teachers to bring in their own white boards. The less concerned teachers either just read from the text or in some cases, napped during class.

And the textbooks were massively out of date. Lou's history textbook only went up to 1992. Apparently, the school district didn't think anything important happened after that date.

Despite all of that, Lou looked forward to going to school. She'd managed to get into some AP classes, which were definitely better than the regular classes. The teachers actually seemed to care.

A lot of other students looked at high school like doing time - they just needed to make it through.

Not Lou - she knew school was her ticket to better things. Usually, that meant she was first in class - sitting in the front and ready to go.

But not today.

Students streamed by Lou but she didn't pay them any attention. She hadn't slept well after Jen had left. She'd ended up pacing the halls and jumping up at the smallest sound. She'd propped the front door back up and pushed a dresser against it as a barrier. But she kept imagining someone creeping through.

This morning, she felt like a complete idiot. Why had she let the woman's crazy talk get to her?

But at least Jen had brought her library books back. Lou smiled a little when she thought of the money tucked safely away in her pocket. It wasn't much, but right now, every penny counted.

The bell rang and a couple of kids dashed into classrooms. Others continued their slow walk down the hall, either not concerned about being late, okay with being late, or skipping class all together.

Lou fell in the last category. She was supposed to go to Computer Science but there was no way she could listen to Mrs. Huckelford drone on about word processing. Besides, Lou had been computer literate since she was a kid. Mrs. Huckelford, meanwhile, couldn't answer any question not addressed by their textbook.

Lou slid into the stairwell. There was a music room on the third floor that was slowly turning into a storage closet. It should be empty and hopefully, she could get a little sleep.

Hitching her backpack on her shoulder, Lou began to climb. She went over the scene from the house yesterday. The woman might be crazy but she certainly could fight. If Lou hadn't been in the middle of it, she would have been really impressed.

Too late, Lou recognized that there were people on the landing between the second and third floors. She stopped in mid-step taking in the scene. Bobby Kiender and two of his minions, Sal and Brick, had a girl cornered. Bobby was nineteen but only a junior.

He had the girl pinned against the wall. Sal and Brick leaned against the wall watching.

Lou recognized the girl - Ann Marie Sonner. She was a freshman. Nice kid - smart. No way she was voluntarily hanging out with these three.

Ann Marie's terrified gaze latched onto Lou's and pleaded for help.

Brick stepped away from the wall, hitting Bobby on the arm. "Company."

Bobby looked over. "Get lost, bitch."

Yesterday, Lou probably would have. Or at least she would have run and gotten help. But today, something was different. She just couldn't leave Ann Marie behind.

Lou stepped onto the landing. "Leave her alone." The words were good. The tremor in her voice was not.

Brick let out a laugh. "Oh yeah? And why's that, sugar lips?"

Bobby nodded his head toward her. "Take care of her."

Brick smirked. He walked over to her, reaching out a giant paw. Lou stepped to the side, smacked the hand out of the way, and hit him in the face with an open palm.

Blood burst from his nose. Brick crashed to his knees. "She broke my nose," he cried, surprise more than anger in his voice.

Sal ran for her. Lou waited until the last second and then stepped to the side. Turning, she put one hand on Sal's back and pushed. With a scream, he tumbled down the flight of stairs.

Lou stared at Sal who lay in a heap one flight down. *How the hell-?*

Too late, she noticed Bobby coming up behind her. He wrapped his arms around her and jabbed a knife into her ribs. She screamed in pain as she elbowed him in the ribs, feeling one of them break. Now it was his turn to yell in pain. Lou grabbed one of his pinkies and yanked it back. He yelped releasing her.

Lou turned, anger racing through her. She grabbed Bobby by the throat and threw him against the wall. He slammed into it and collapsed to the ground, leaving a little indent in the wall, bits of plaster crashing down around him.

Lou stared at him in disbelief. *How did I do that?*

Brick backed away from her, all but tripping over his feet to get away. Bobby shook his head like some cartoon character and Sal was moaning down on the stairs.

Ann Marie walked up to her, shaking. "Lou?"

Lou turned to her, pushing her shock away. "Are you okay?"

Ann Marie threw her arms around her. "Thank you."

Lou returned the hug as Jen's words replayed in her mind. *The Fallen are reborn time and time again and live out their lives with their powers.*

Ann Marie looked at Lou's shirt, where Bobby had stabbed her. "You've been hurt. I'll get help." She ran off before Lou could think to stop her.

Lou looked at her side, pulling up her shirt to get a better view. The wound had stopped bleeding. She watched in disbelief as the wound began to stitch close.

She felt lightheaded. She reached out for the wall. *Jen wasn't crazy. I am one of them. The park wasn't a fluke.*

Her chest clutched as she remembered the rest of what Jen had said. She scrambled to her feet, fear crashing through her.

Charlotte.

CHAPTER 12

Lou ran all the way home. But she had to make a concerted effort to run at a normal speed.

Her mind still couldn't wrap around what had happened in the stairwell or what was happening to her. She was fast, strong, and healed really fast. Jen was right. She was one of them.

Lou had run into Ann Marie at the bottom of the stairwell and promised her she was fine - that the cut hadn't been deep. Ann Marie had been skeptical but she had promised not to say anything to anyone about Lou's involvement.

Lou turned the corner onto her street. An electric tingle rolled through her. Her head whipped up. Jen stood leaning against her Tahoe in Lou's driveway.

"What are you doing here?" Lou asked. Her tone was gruff, but relief flowed through her at the sight of the tall agent. She had been debating whether or not to call her the whole run home.

Jen straightened up. "I brought some supplies to fix your front door and I wanted to check on you. See how you're doing."

Lou nodded. "I'm okay."

Jen took a step forward, her eyes narrowing. "Why are you home so early? Did something happen?"

"No. Why?"

Jen reached out lightning fast and grabbed Lou's arm. She nodded at the dark stain on Lou's jacket. "That's blood. You didn't have it yesterday." Jen flipped open Lou's jacket. "Your shirt's ripped."

Lou looked down at the blood, feeling a little lightheaded again. "How about if we sit down?"

Jen looked like she wanted to say something, but she just nodded, her mouth a tight line.

Lou led Jen up the drive and around the back of the house. She took a seat on the top of the porch steps.

Jen leaned against the railing at the bottom of the steps. "Tell me what happened."

Lou shook her head, imagining the fight again. "A girl at school had a run in with some not so good guys. I helped a little."

Jen raised an eyebrow. "You okay?"

"Yeah, but um, I got stabbed."

Jen looked at her, not at all alarmed.

Somehow Jen's lack of response bolstered Lou's own calm. "But um, it healed."

Jen nodded. "Probably in a couple of seconds, right?"

"Yeah, I uh -" Lou put her head in her hands. "Am I really one of those things you said?"

"A Fallen? Yes."

"So I can't get hurt?"

"Oh you can get hurt. I'm guessing that stab wound hurt quite a bit. You'll just heal quickly from injuries."

Letting out a breath, Lou felt better. Okay. She could handle this. It might actually be kind of cool, having superpowers. But she remembered what her Grandmother had said about fallen angels.

"But, they fell from God's grace, right? They disobeyed God. They're cursed. I'm cursed."

Jen climbed the stairs and sat down. She looked Lou right in the eyes and shook her head. "No. I don't believe that. I don't think there is anything that you can't come back from. What you do here and now determines the person you are - not what you did eons ago."

"Eons ago?" Lou whispered, pulling her gaze from Jen's and looking at the overgrown backyard. Was this for real?

"Yes. Eons ago," Jen said.

Standing up, Lou walked along the porch before she leaned against the railing and stared at the back fence. "I just-." She shook her head. "I don't even know what to say to that."

Moving next to her Jen, Jen looked out over the yard as well. "I know. It's a lot. I just learned about my nature a few months ago. I knew about my abilities since I was younger than you. But I didn't know why I had them. I didn't know what they meant."

"Who told you?"

Jen gave her a little smile. "A friend. She knew what I was. She'd had dealings with people like me."

"So she's not one?"

"Actually, she is. But she's a very unique one. And that's a much longer story that I would be happy to tell you someday, but I think maybe we should focus on you for today."

Lou nodded, wanting to hear the story but at the same time knowing her mind wasn't ready for it. She was still trying to process what she'd learned about herself. "Yeah. I think maybe I'm enough for today."

CHAPTER 13

Jen lifted the two by four she'd picked up at the hardware store out of the back of her truck and carried it up the porch steps. While Lou was at school, she'd stopped by and taken measurements. Then she'd had them cut the wood to size at the store.

She'd also grabbed the tools she thought she'd need for the job. She hadn't exactly been prepared to do home repairs on this trip but like usual she made do with what she had.

After leaning the wood against the opening, Jen double-checked that she was lined up correctly and began to hammer it in.

Lou sat on the bottom step in the hallway across from her. "Where'd you learn to fix a door?"

Smiling at her over her shoulder, Jen said, "I've picked up a lot of things over the years."

"You mean as an agent?"

Jen laughed. "No. Actually that's a recent career change. My regular job is as an archaeologist. Being in the middle of nowhere, you tend to get good at a lot of skills. There's no other choice. Hand me that Phillips screwdriver, would you?"

Lou stared at the tools before grabbing the correct screwdriver and handing it over. "So you're not an archaeologist right now?"

Jen finished screwing the hinges into the top of the frame and pocketed the screwdriver. She hadn't thought of it in those terms before. What was she now?

She couldn't imagine disappearing into a dig site right now or sitting down to write up research findings - not with everything that was going on. "You know that's a good question. And to be honest, I don't have an answer for that."

Thoughts of Danny and the search for the other kids popped into her mind. "There's a project I'm working on that requires all my time right now."

"Am I part of that project?"

Jen nodded. "I'm looking for kids like you, like me. Making sure they're safe. That no one else can get to them."

"You mean like that other group you were talking about."

Measuring out where to place the lower hinges, Jen nodded. "Yes."

"So who is this other group?"

Jen paused. How should she explain that evil? "They are actually just like us. Except for the small fact that they are more interested in ruling humanity than co-existing with them."

"Ruling them? Like what, kings?"

"Actually, I think they probably consider themselves more like supreme rulers."

Lou looked away and Jen wondered if she should have softened the truth a little bit.

Lou looked back at her after a moment. "You said before that Charlotte could be in trouble."

"This group's MO is to isolate a candidate by taking out members of their family. You might not be in trouble. They might not have caught onto the fact that you have any abilities. If that's the case, then no, your sister is not in any danger from them. But if they have, then she is."

Lou rested her head on her hand, her eyes troubled.

"Look there's a chance that you're not on their radar yet," Jen said. "But the fact is, I found you. And if I could, they could."

Lou looked at her for a long moment. "So what do you do if you find one of us?"

Jen paused. "Actually, you're the first one I've found like this. But there are others we found that were already in the recruitment process."

Lou interrupted. "The recruitment process?"

Straightening from her work, Jen stopped what she was doing and went to sit next to Lou. "These guys, they grab or recruit kids. And then they set them up in a training facility. They teach them how to fight and they keep the strongest."

"What do they do with the weakest?"

Jen looked away, but she knew Lou deserved the truth. "They kill them."

Lou sucked in a breath, her eyes wide. "What did you do with them?"

"We set them up at a safe location. They go to school, have new identities. If you want, you can go there, too."

Lou glanced up the stairs.

Jen had seen Lou go up before to check on Charlotte. Lou's sister was a mess right now. There was no doubt about that. But she was also the only family Lou had left.

Lou looked back at Jen. "I can't leave Charlotte."

"I wouldn't expect you to. We'll bring you both in," Jen said.

Lou sighed. "She won't ever go for that."

Lou went quiet and Jen let her have silence for her internal debate. Finally, Lou spoke. "Can you give me a couple of days to talk her into it?"

Jen looked around Lou's house. The place should probably be condemned. And there wasn't really a good way to shore it up if anyone came for Lou - too many windows and doors. Although, Jen reasoned, they did tend to only talk on the first visit.

But Jen and her friends had discovered two camps so far. They were disrupting the way things normally worked. Who knew how that would upset the balance? She shook her head. "I can't leave you alone for that long."

Lou nodded back at her glumly.

"How about if I put you guys up at the hotel I'm staying at? I'll set you guys up with your own room, right next to me or maybe we'll even get a suite. You'll have your own space, but I'll be nearby, just in case."

Lou's eyes grew big at the idea, a smile spreading across her face. "Seriously?"

Jen realized that back in the day she would have been just as thrilled. Clean sheets. Big shower. Cable TV - it would have been a little slice of heaven. Jen smiled. "Yes. Seriously."

Lou glanced over at Jen, one eyebrow raised. "Why now, though? You left us alone last night."

"Actually I didn't. I slept in my car a few houses down."

"I didn't sense you."

"I stayed just far enough away to be out of your range. I'm learning your tricks," Jen said with a grin.

Lou returned the smile. "Okay. Now we just need to convince my sister."

CHAPTER 14

Lou woke up and stretched, not having slept so well in years. Jen had gotten them a two-bedroom suite. The bedroom was big with plenty of room for two queen beds, a giant flat screen TV, and a bathroom twice the size of her bedroom at home. Outside the bedroom was a full living room and kitchen and another bedroom where Jen was staying.

Lou glanced over to where her sister slept. She had been surprised at how quickly Charlotte had agreed. But maybe she shouldn't have been. It was like a little mini-vacation. Even Charlotte could appreciate that.

Last night, she and Charlotte had each taken really long showers. Charlotte had even taken a bubble bath. Then they had ordered room service and stayed up late watching movies.

Lou smiled. It was like she had gotten her sister back.

Quietly, Lou grabbed her clothes from the chair next to the bed and got changed. Grabbing her shoes, she let herself out of the room, careful to not wake Charlotte. Lou turned around and saw Jen sitting at the kitchen table, breakfast already waiting.

Jen smiled. "There you are. Charlotte still sleeping?"

Lou nodded, the aroma of pancakes pulling her to the table. "Any chance some of those are for me?"

"They all are. I just ate."

Lou took a seat, pouring a mound of syrup on her plate. *Oh this is going to be a good day.*

And actually it was. Lou sat through her classes, a smile on her face. She felt good. She caught Ann Marie's puzzled looks a few times but just shrugged them off. At the end of the day, Lou had to keep herself from skipping down the hall. For once, life had possibility.

The buzz of electricity that ran through her as she pushed through the main doors told Lou that Jen was waiting. Spying Jen's Tahoe, Lou headed over and hopped in the passenger seat. Charlotte was in the back.

Lou glanced back with a grin. "Hey Charlotte."

Charlotte didn't even look at her, just kept looking straight ahead.

Lou's mood dimmed a little. "Charlotte?"

Charlotte turned her head and looked out the window.

Lou glanced over at Jen.

Jen shrugged. "She wanted to stay at the hotel. But I wasn't comfortable leaving her there alone."

The car ride back to the hotel was uncomfortable with Charlotte acting like a pouty three-year old. As soon as they pulled up to the hotel, Charlotte was out of the car. She walked into the lobby, her back straight.

Jen sighed as she came around the car to join Lou on the sidewalk. "Well, this is fun."

"I'm sorry," Lou said. "She just doesn't like being told what to do."

"I know. But I think she's also jonesing for a hit, which is the bigger problem."

Lou knew Jen was right. She liked to tell herself that all her sister used was pot, but she'd seen the track marks. She knew better than that.

Jen put a hand on Lou's arm. "I know someone who can help

her. Get her into a good rehab. Do you want me to make some calls?"

Lou looked over to where her sister had disappeared into an elevator. "Yeah. But I'm not sure I can talk her into it."

"Try."

"I will."

They headed up to the suite in silence. Jen let them in just in time to see Charlotte disappear into the shared bedroom and slam the door.

Lou winced, embarrassed. She looked at Jen. "I'm sorry. She just-."

Jen held up a hand. "You have nothing to apologize for. Why don't you go talk to her? I'll make arrangements for rehab." Jen paused. "There are some that will take her even if she doesn't want to go. Do you know what I mean by that?"

Lou nodded, imagining her sister getting dragged out of the hotel. She took a shuddering breath.

"Can you handle that?" Jen asked.

Lou looked at the closed bedroom door. If it meant getting her sister back, for real this time, then yes she could handle it. She nodded. "Yeah. Set it up."

Jen pulled out her phone, heading for the other bedroom. "Okay. It'll probably take a day or two to get everything in place."

Lou nodded and then walked over to the bedroom door. Steeling herself, she knocked. "Charlotte? It's me."

No answer.

"I'm coming in." Lou turned the knob.

Charlotte lay on the bed with the TV on mute across from her.

Lou sat on the other bed. "Hey. Is everything okay?"

Charlotte glared at her out of the corner of her eyes. "Okay? The warden won't let me go anywhere."

Lou sighed. "Charlotte, we talked about this. It's not safe right now. Jen's going to get us a new place. Somewhere we can have a fresh start."

"Who the hell is this bitch? And why do you believe her? She's not family."

"I know. But Charlotte, this is our shot. We can have a life - a real one. I can go to college and you can get clean-." Lou clamped her mouth shut, wanting to yank the words back. She'd never mentioned her sister's drug use before.

Charlotte sat up, her eyes narrowed. "What did you say?"

"Nothing. I just said we could start over."

"So what, this is some sort of intervention?" Charlotte's voice got louder.

Lou put up her hands. "No. It's not that. This is about us getting a shot at a normal life."

Charlotte looked away. When she turned back, the anger was gone, but the sly look Lou knew all too well was on her face. "You're right. This is our chance. And we should take it."

Lou nodded slowly, waiting.

"But I think it's only fair that if I do this for you, I get to say good-bye to my friends first."

Lou hesitated.

Charlotte walked over to Lou, pulling her into a hug. Lou breathed in deep, enjoying the feel of her sister holding her.

Charlotte took Lou's face in her hands, kissing her on the forehead. "Let me just say my good-byes and then we go together. Okay? We can start our new life without having to look back."

Lou wanted to say no. Part of her knew she was being manipulated. But this was the old Charlotte, her beautiful sister. She found herself nodding before she could say anything. "Um, Jen's in her room. If you want to go, it needs to be now."

Charlotte hugged her. "Great. I'll see you tonight. We'll watch some more movies, okay?"

Lou nodded, but her sister was already out the door. It closed behind her. "Yeah. See you later," she said to nobody.

Lou sank onto the bed, clutching a pillow to her chest. *It will be all right. Charlotte will only be gone for a few hours and then we'll start over - just the two of us.*

She stared at the door while the ridiculous daydream of Charlotte re-appearing and telling her she didn't want to go played out in her mind. Finally she pulled her gaze, dropped her head to the pillow and let the tears fall.

CHAPTER 15

Lou spent the rest of the afternoon with Jen. They played cards - watched some TV. Lou did her homework. Jen had asked about Charlotte but Lou had covered for her, saying she was asleep.

At six, they'd ordered room service. The steak had been good, but Lou barely tasted it. Where was Charlotte? Why wasn't she back yet?

"You okay?" Jen asked.

"Yeah. I mean, no. I'm not feeling so well. I think I'll go lie down."

Jen narrowed her eyes. "You want me to get you anything?"

Lou stood up, avoiding her eyes. "Uh, no. It's okay."

"Well, if Charlotte's up, tell her she's welcome to come in here so you can get some sleep."

"Yeah, I will. Thanks." Lou fled to the other room, quietly opening the bedroom door in case Charlotte had somehow returned without telling her. But the room was empty.

Lou's stomach plunged to her feet. She pulled out her cell phone and dialed. A buzzing sounded from the desk.

Lou walked over to it and pulled up a notepad.

Charlotte's phone hopped along the desktop.

Lou grabbed it. *Damn it Charlotte.*

CHAPTER 16

Pascha Bukin walked down the street in southern Detroit. He slumped his shoulders, shortening his four foot ten frame when he saw two guys standing outside the gas station at the corner. Each drank from a bottle wrapped in a brown paper bag.

One wore a tank top even though the night was cool and the other wore a grimy grey t-shirt. Both needed better belts to pull up their pants. Tank Top nudged T-shirt as Pascha passed.

Pascha smiled trying hard not to laugh. He turned down the alley next to the station, knowing it dead-ended. *Time for some fun.*

He'd been searching for a potential, but she'd up and left her home. No one had seen her, although in a neighborhood like this he hadn't expected anyone to notice.

But then he'd heard through the grapevine that the potential's sister had a drug problem and tended to score around here. He'd been prowling this area for hours and he was growing annoyed. He was not a patient man. Having nothing to show for his time did not sit well with him.

Well, not nothing, he thought with a smile. He pictured the woman as he'd left her. He had managed to work in a little fun.

But he was growing bored again. And the neighborhood wasn't helping. He walked past an overflowing dumpster with a grimace.

The scuffle of a shoe brought him back to the present. "Hey you."

It was hard not to laugh. Pascha turned around slowly. "Me?"

Tank Top smirked. "Yeah you. You need to give us your money."

Pascha took a step toward them, his eyes large. He tilted his head to the side looking over both of the men. "Really? Why?"

Tank Top pulled out a knife. "'Cause we're going to mess you up if you don't."

Pretending to ponder his words for a moment, Pascha said, "You know, I think I'm going to have to choose the fight. I like my money."

"Stupid choice, little man," T-shirt growled.

Pascha stiffened. "Don't call me little."

Tank Top smirked. "Aw, little man doesn't like being called little."

T-shirt laughed. "Sure thing, little man."

Going still, Pascha tracked each of the men as they tried to move on him. Tank Top lunged at him, the knife aimed for Pascha's chest.

With a leap out of the way, Pascha wrapped his arm around Tank Top's neck. At the same time, he ran up the alley wall. Flipping over Tank Top, he kept his arm around his neck. With a yell, Tank Top landed with a grunt on his back, his head thudding against the ground.

T-shirt ran at him. "Asshole!"

Waiting until the last second, Pascha stepped to the side, throwing a palm heel at the man's face. The man slammed to a stop, his eyes rolled back into his head and he dropped.

Tank Top started to crawl away.

But Pascha walked around him, standing in his way.

Tank Top reared back. "I'm sorry, man. We didn't mean nothing."

Pascha knelt down and patted him on the cheek. "Of course

you did. You meant to hurt me. Didn't really work out that well for you, though, did it?"

"What are you? Some kind of vigilante?"

Laughing hard, Pascha held his stomach. "Vigilante? Oh god that's good." He wiped at his eyes.

Tank Top cringed away.

Pascha snatched the knife from the ground and twirled it, before yanking Tank Top back toward him. "Oh come back here. And to answer your question - No, I am not a vigilante. *I am a god.*"

He plunged the knife into the man's throat. Tank Top gurgled as the blood poured from his neck and out of his mouth.

Pascha knelt down staring into the man's eyes. They begged Pascha for help and then like that - they stopped asking for anything.

As he sat back, Pascha titled his head. That moment of death always intrigued him. What was it that disappeared in that second between life and oblivion?

He took the man's shirt and wiped his fingerprints off the blade, dropping it next to the body.

Pascha straightened, his blood humming. Death was his drug of choice - the power over life and death was more potent than anything that could be shot up someone's arm.

He walked down the alley and headed for the grocery store a few blocks over - the two men already forgotten.

A few minutes later, he was across the street from the store. He settled onto a bench to wait. He'd heard drugs could be scored here as well. Pulling his candy bar from his pocket, he sighed. What a waste of his talents.

A short time later, Pascha had begun to grow restless. There weren't many people about. Only three in fact had gone into the store in a half hour. This was the worst part of these assignments - the waiting.

A movement down the street drew his attention. He squinted

trying to make out the person. Long hair, slim build - definitely a woman.

Pascha straightened to get a better look. The woman stepped into the glow of the streetlight.

Pascha smiled, his voice whisper soft. "Hello Charlotte."

CHAPTER 17

Jen flipped through the channels looking for something to occupy her time. She'd called Henry a few hours ago. He was arranging for the rehab for Charlotte. He said he'd have it set up for tomorrow.

Jen glanced at the closed bedroom door. It was quiet. *Maybe they both fell asleep.*

Jen sighed. She was not looking forward to the confrontation with Charlotte tomorrow but she also knew it was the best thing for Charlotte - and for Lou.

Thinking of the young girl, Jen looked back at Lou's door. She had seemed a little off tonight, but she'd been through a lot in the last few days. She probably just needed a little time.

Jen's head turned toward Lou's door as she heard footsteps. Her eyes flicked to the clock. 10:45. *Something's wrong.*

Jen sprang off the couch as Lou opened the door. "Lou? What's going on?"

In the dim light, Lou's face looked paler, the fear and innocence more noticeable. "It's Charlotte. She's gone."

"What? When?"

Lou looked at her feet. "She wanted to go say good-bye to some people and then she was going to come right back."

Jen swallowed down the curses that wanted to escape her lips. "What time was that?"

Lou glanced up at her, her eyes big. "Right after school?"

Shit. She'd been gone for almost six hours. "Lou grab, your jacket. Let's go find your sister."

Lou sprinted back into her room, a hopeful look replacing the fear on her face.

Jen hated seeing it. She grabbed the car keys from the table and strode toward the door of the suite.

Because Jen had the distinct feeling, there was absolutely nothing to be hopeful about.

CHAPTER 18

Jen drove down the darkened street, chastising herself. Why the hell hadn't she checked in on Charlotte? She'd let her go under her watch.

She clenched the steering wheel, guilt eating at her. Her eyes scanned every person on the sidewalk. *Come on Charlotte, where are you?*

Jen made a right. They'd been tracing and re-tracing all of Charlotte's haunts for two hours. Jen had personally inspected over six drug dens. Each place had made her skin crawl a little bit more.

They'd stopped once for a snack and some drinks. While Lou was waiting for the food, Jen had put in a call to Detroit PD asking them to put out a BOLO on Charlotte. But nothing had come through there either.

Jen wasn't sure what else to do. She had security in the hotel on alert to call if Charlotte showed up.

Maybe she should call Danny to see if he could tap into the city's cameras - do some sort of facial recognition search. Although Jen was pretty sure the areas Charlotte was most likely to go to would not be known for their high security.

Lou's voice cut into her thoughts. "She's done this before, you know - run off. She'll be back. It'll probably only be a couple of days or something."

Jen nodded, but didn't say anything, knowing it was Lou's nerves, not her logic talking.

Jen's phone beeped and she looked down. Her gut clenched - Detroit P.D. She pulled over and put the car in park. "Lou, I need to take this."

Stepping out of the car, Jen was careful to close the door. Once she was a few steps from the car, she answered the phone. "Agent Witt."

"This is Officer Connolly with DPD. My sergeant said to give you a call. I have a body here that might match the BOLO you put out."

Jen looked over at the car. Lou's gaze was focused on her. *Damn.*

Turning her back to the car, Jen walked a little farther away. "What was the cause of death?"

"Throat cut. Pretty deep. Guy wasn't taking any chances."

Jen closed her eyes. *No.* "Can you send me a picture?"

"Sure thing."

A few seconds later, her phone chimed. Jen clicked open the text. Charlotte's pale face stared back at her, a few splashes of blood across it.

Jen closed her eyes. *Damn it, Charlotte. Why didn't you just stay in the hotel?* She opened her eyes and let out a breath. "Yeah. That's her."

The officer made a couple more comments about claiming the body and making an official ID but Jen tuned it out, trying to figure out what she was going to say to Lou. Finishing up with the officer, she turned to the car. She still didn't know what she was going to say.

But as she caught Lou's eyes through the windshield, she realized she wouldn't have to say anything.

Tears streamed down the girl's face.

Lou already knew.

CHAPTER 19

Jen sat next to Lou on the edge of the swimming pool at the back of the hotel. Their feet dangled a few inches above the water. Jen hadn't let Lou identify the body, even though Lou had demanded to see Charlotte. Jen would take care of that. Lou didn't need that image in her head.

"My Mom loved to read," Lou said. "*Little Women* was one of her favorite books. That's where I got my name."

"And Charlotte Bronte for your sister."

Lou nodded, giving Jen a watery smile. She wiped at a tear that rolled down her cheek. "Charlotte use to write these great stories. She'd leave them for me and Mom to read. I'd wake up some mornings, and there'd be this little present next to my pillow. In my favorite, she wrote about these two sisters who were girl detectives who uncovered a dog stealing ring in the city. It was really good."

"She stopped writing?"

Lou nodded. "Yeah. When Mom died, she stopped. She never wrote another story. She never did a lot of things again. My sister died that night too and this stranger came to live in her place."

"I'm really sorry, Lou."

Lou shrugged, trying to sound tough. "I always knew it was

going to end bad for her. But I kept hoping that maybe my sister would come back. She did a little when Grandma died. She took care of me. I thought-." She shook her head, biting her lip.

"You thought she'd stay that way."

Lou took a shuddering breath. "Yeah. But then she lost her job, hooked back up with her old friends, and like that," Lou snapped her fingers, "she was gone again. When that happened, I knew my sister was really gone. I'd never see her again."

Jen felt helpless and guilty. Charlotte had been killed and Jen hadn't even known she was gone.

Lou swiped at her tears. "I mean it's stupid, right? Charlotte's barely known I was around for the last few years. So I don't even know why I'm crying."

Jen watched Lou out of the corner of her eye. Lou was trying to be strong. Jen knew that mindset, because it was hers. Pretend nothing was wrong. Don't let anyone in.

She also knew that Lou felt like her world was falling apart. Jen hesitated for only a moment. "You're crying because she was your sister. You're crying because you love her. You're crying because her death means the sister you grew up with, the one you loved, is really not coming back now."

Lou looked over at Jen, her bottom lip trembling. She nodded slowly. "Yeah."

The silence stretched between them. Jen wished her own Mom was here. Not her biological Mom because even when she was around, she wasn't exactly affectionate. But her adopted Mom. She'd know what to do. Martha Witt always seemed to know what someone needed.

She would hug Lou and tell her everything would be all right. And when Jen's mom hugged you, you believed her. She had a powerful hug.

Jen didn't have that power and right now she'd trade all her other skills for the ability to make this one girl feel less alone.

Jen had asked her Mom once why it was that people seemed to respond to her so well. Her Mom gave a little laugh. 'It's simple honey. People can feel caring. And everyone can use a little more love in their life.'

Reaching over, Jen pulled Lou into her shoulder. "I'm so sorry Lou," she said, her heart in every word.

Lou went stiff at first. Then she turned into Jen's embrace. Lou's shoulders began to shake and then she cried so hard, Jen worried she'd break in two.

Jen hugged her tight, wishing she could do more - and blaming herself for not getting Lou and Charlotte out of Detroit sooner.

Lou sobbed in Jen's arms like her whole world was ending.

And Jen had nothing to say to that grief.

Because it was true - Lou's whole world had changed and the new one she had just stepped into was scary as hell.

CHAPTER 20

JEN CLOSED over the door to Lou's bedroom, not wanting to shut it the whole way in case Lou needed her. Lou had cried herself out at the water. She'd been as pliant as a doll since then.

Jen hated that Lou was going through this. She hated that she hadn't been able to protect Lou from Charlotte and Charlotte from herself.

Blowing out a breath, she pulled out her phone. She'd give anything to talk to Laney right now.

But she knew Laney was with Jake and those two had gotten very little time alone in the last few months. She and Henry had decided to keep them out of this particular mission if they could. They had enough on their plates. And if Jen called Laney, Laney would on a plane out here as fast as she could manage.

No - calling Laney wasn't an option.

Jen looked at the clock and knew Henry had a conference call with Japan in a few minutes. She could call Kati but she was worried about how Kati was handling all of this. She wasn't used to violence and superpowers. Jen didn't want to add any more worries onto her.

So she flipped a mental coin and then dialed.

Her brother Jordan Witt answered in a few seconds. "Little sister. I was just thinking about you."

"Good things I hope."

"Always. I was going to see if you wanted to meet me and Mike for dinner tomorrow." Mike was Jen's other brother and Jordan's twin. They were identical from their athletic, six-foot frames to their pale blonde hair and bright blue eyes.

Jen smiled. "Love to, but it'll be a bit of a trip for you both. I'm in Detroit."

"Detroit? What are you doing there?"

Jen quickly filled Jordan in on the situation with Lou. She took a water bottle from the mini bar and slid down the wall, sitting cross-legged on the floor. "So now, this poor girl is alone. And she just had her whole world torn apart."

Jordan was quiet on the other line for a beat. "I'm guessing this is cutting a little close to home."

Jen let out a breath. "I'm trying not to let it, but when I see her, I see me - I mean, I had you guys. She doesn't have anyone."

"From the way you're talking, I'm thinking she's got you now in her corner. Which I guess means she gets the rest of us, too." He paused for a few seconds. "What about whoever killed her sister? Any leads?"

"No. A junkie gets killed and the cops aren't exactly pulling out all the stops to track down the doer. It'll probably never be solved. But I'm going down to the DPD tomorrow."

"You'll find them. I have faith. But what's the plan with Lou?"

Jen looked over at the closed bedroom door. Even without the super hearing, she could hear Lou's cries. Apparently Lou hadn't been quite as cried out as Jen had thought. "I'm getting her out of here. As soon as possible."

CHAPTER 21

HENRY PULLED to the side of the road a little before the entrance of the hotel where Jen was staying.

What am I doing? He thought for the umpteenth time since he'd made the rash decision to come visit Jen.

He'd been in Toronto when his conference call to Japan had been cancelled. He thought he'd swing by and visit Jen. But now he worried about how that would look. *What am I going to say? I was two hundred miles away and decided to stop by?*

He rubbed his hands over his face. What was happening to him? He was known for his ability to make quick decisions - to read situations with unerring accuracy. And yet when it came to Jen, he'd turned into an infatuated schoolboy.

He put the car back into drive. *Well, I'm here. Time to do this.* He pulled back into traffic.

A few minutes later, he'd left the car with the valet and was in the elevator on the way up to Jen's room.

As he walked down the hall, he realized he probably should have called first. He paused and looked back down the hall. Should he head back downstairs and then call?

Henry shook his head. If Jen saw him right now, she'd tell him to get his act together. He smiled at the thought and continued down the hall, now anxious to see her.

Taking a breath he knocked on Jen's door, feeling the familiar tingle run along his skin.

"Who is it?" Jen called.

"Um, it's Henry."

"Henry?" Jen undid the bolt and the door swung open.

"Um hi. I was nowhere in the neighborhood and thought I'd stop by."

Jen looked at him for a moment.

Henry paused, seeing the strain on her face and the unshed tears in her eyes. "Jen? What happened?"

"Oh, Henry, I think I messed up." Jen stepped forward and Henry closed his arms around her as her tears fell.

Henry rested his chin on the top of her head. *Yeah. Coming to see her was the right call.*

CHAPTER 22

THE NEXT MORNING, Jen dropped Lou off at school. Jen had tried to talk her out of going but Lou insisted. She said she had an AP review she couldn't miss.

"Who was over last night?" Lou asked when Jen pulled up in front of the high school.

Those were the first words she had spoken in over an hour.

Jen looked over at her confused and then realized Lou would have felt Henry enter the room. "My friend, Henry."

Henry had stayed for a few hours last night and they had talked the whole time. There was something about Henry that made Jen feel safe - and something more that she didn't want to dwell on right now.

She'd told him everything about Charlotte and Lou. And he'd listened. He hadn't given her advice or told her what she should do. He just listened and asked what he could do to help. She knew he wasn't just being polite. Anything she wanted, he would make happen.

As he asked, she realized there was one thing she wanted: her brother Jordan here. There were only a handful of people Jen trusted to watch Lou. And Jordan was at the top of that list.

Jen wouldn't be able to watch Lou at school and follow up on the investigation into Charlotte's death. Jordan had been a Navy SEAL for years and had gone to work for the Chandler Group when he'd decided to leave the service.

Henry picked up the phone immediately and found someone to take over for Jordan on his current assignment. He'd be arriving later today. Henry had also arranged for a Chandler operative to be stationed outside the school until Jordan arrived.

Then Henry had had to leave. They had stood awkwardly in the door, saying good night. But then Henry's phone had rung and he'd had to answer it. He'd headed down the hall with a look Jen couldn't quite read. - Remorse maybe? Regret?

"Oh," Lou murmured, looking back out the window.

Jen glanced over at her trying to come up with something to say and failing.

Lou reached for the door handle.

"Are you sure you're up for this?" Jen asked, needing to try again to keep Lou home.

Lou nodded, not looking at her. "Yeah. I'll see you later."

Lou slowly got out of the car, closing the door behind her. She walked up the steps of the school and disappeared through the main doors without looking back.

Jen watched the other students go in and out the doors. Jen slammed her palm into the steering wheel. *Damn it.*

She felt useless. Lou was grieving and there was no way for Jen to prevent her from feeling that pain. She'd just have to get through. This morning, Jen had brought up leaving town but Jen wasn't sure Lou had even heard her. Jen had dropped the topic, promising herself she'd talk to Lou this afternoon and make sure she understood the need to leave.

The only thing she could really do for Lou right now was find out who'd killed Charlotte. At this point, they weren't even sure she had been killed by a Fallen. After all, murders were not that uncommon in Lou's neighborhood. Charlotte's death could just be a horrible coincidence.

Shaking herself, Jen put the car back in gear, glancing at the clock. She'd need to move.

CHAPTER 23

It might not be related, Jen reminded herself as she pushed through the doors of the Detroit Police Department fifteen minutes later. The smells of BO and urine were now joined by the dual smells of vomit and bleach.

Even lovelier, Jen thought as she headed to the front desk.

Unlike last time she'd visited, this time she had to wade her way through about a dozen people adding to the noise and smell of the place.

The sergeant at the desk, though, was a much more efficient one. She handed a paper to an officer behind her, took notes on a citizen leaning forward who was complaining about the kids who'd tagged his garage, and held up a finger at a woman who kept trying to get her attention. Even with all that chaos surrounding her, the sergeant spied Jen when she was still a few feet away. "Agent Witt?"

Jen stepped to the desk, flashing her badge with a nod.

The sergeant nudged her head to the right while she reached under the desk and buzzed her in. "They're expecting you down in surveillance. Third door on your right."

"Thanks." Jen headed past the desk and into the bullpen behind, leaving the sergeant to her juggling act.

The bullpen was also a beehive of activity. A couple of officers nodded at her. A few uniforms just straight up checked her out.

Jen ignored them all as she made her way down the hall. She knocked on the closed door of the surveillance room.

"It's open," yelled a male voice.

Jen opened the door and was faced with a room jammed with electronics equipment. Old keyboards and towers of electronics Jen couldn't identify were stacked on top of each other like some homage to old technology. Racks of other equipment and boxes of wires encircled the room.

Jen carefully made her way through the maze. "Um hello?"

A short man with a slim build in his forties appeared from behind a tower of what looked like jumbled wires. "Hi there. You must be Agent Witt. I'm Juan Riley."

Jen raised her eyebrows at the name.

He smiled. "Mom's from Puerto Rico. Dad's family is from Dublin." He waved her forward. "Come on back. I've got you cued up."

Jen smiled following him back. Juan was not what she'd expected. He was pretty friendly for an electronics guy. She'd picture someone who barely got out of his cave. Actually she realized with a start she was expecting someone like Dr. Dominic Radcliffe, the brilliant agoraphobe who worked for the Chandler Group. Maybe Jen was the one who needed to get out more.

Jen followed Juan to a long table pushed against the back wall. A monitor sat there with black and white footage paused.

Juan sat down and gestured to the chair next to him. "Have a seat."

Jen did, nodding toward the monitor. "That the grocery store?"

Juan nodded. "Yeah. We got lucky. They actually have a working security camera. Most places just put the cameras up for show. I haven't had a chance to go through it yet."

"All right. Let's see what we've got then."

"It's cued up for around seven. The prelim on the vic suggests she died around 10:30." Juan pressed play.

Onscreen, the picture remained the same. Apparently, the grocer wasn't exactly busy. "I'll fast forward," Juan said.

He hit another button and the time clock in the bottom right began to roll forward faster. Three people entered the store and left, but obviously none were Charlotte.

"Hold on," Jen said as a woman stepped into the frame.

Juan ran the tape at normal speed and Jen got her first good look at Charlotte. She was stumbling a little.

"That her?" Juan asked.

Jen nodded, her eyes on the screen. Charlotte weaved toward the door of the store like she was on the bow of a ship in a storm. The clock read 10:28.

A blur slashed across the screen. All of a sudden, Charlotte was on the ground, convulsing.

Jen felt cold.

Juan frowned and started fidgeting with dials. "Something must be wrong with the tape."

Jen shook her head, dread spreading through her. There was nothing wrong with the video.

"Shit," she murmured.

CHAPTER 24

Lou walked through her high school feeling like she was in a daze. How could Charlotte be dead? She vacillated between thinking it had all been a horrible dream and reality crushing her with the reminder that she was now truly alone in the world.

She'd told Jen she wanted to come in for the AP study session. And there was one during second period, but Lou didn't have any idea what the teacher had said during it. In fact, Mrs. Ingram stopped her after class. "Everything all right?"

Mrs. Ingram's hazel eyes peered at Lou from behind her glasses.

Lou shouldered her backpack, staring past her, not able to meet the concern in her teacher's eyes. "I'm okay."

Mrs. Ingram looked like she wanted to say more but students from her next class walked in the door. Mrs. Ingram glanced over her shoulder. Lou used the distraction to slip past her.

And that had been it for her classes that day. Lou wasn't up to sitting in a class pretending everything was normal - because it wasn't. Everything was so far from normal it was laughable.

She walked up to the music room that she'd been trying to get to when she'd run into Brick and Ann Marie. *Was that just two days ago?*

Lou hopped up on the windowsill and stared out the window. Weariness pulled at her. She leaned her head against the glass. She was too tired to even cry. "Why Charlotte? Why?" she whispered.

At some point she must have fallen asleep because the buzzing of her phone woke her. She glanced at it through heavy eyelids. It was from Jen: Be there in ten minutes.

Lou let her head drop back against the wall, looking at students milling outside in the sunshine. It was wrong. It should be cloudy, raining, maybe even some lightning strikes. Sunshine just made it seem like Charlotte was gone and it didn't matter.

Her mind numb, Lou stared outside for a few more minutes. Finally, she shook herself from her stupor. Sliding off the windowsill, she made her way out of the classroom and through the halls to the front door.

Barely feeling the electrical signal, Lou pushed through the doors and saw Jen standing by the car right out front. A few guys near Jen were trying to get her attention. Jen ignored them.

One kid, egged on by his friends walked up to Jen. *Oh this should be good*, Lou thought. She felt the small smile creep onto her face despite the cloud that seemed to have enveloped her.

"Hey baby. You lookin' good. You'd look even better in my bed."

Jen glanced at him and then away, her expression unchanged.

Undaunted he stepped forward, grabbing his crotch. "I think you need a man who-"

Jen pulled back her jacket to reveal her badge. "Go away."

He paused then smirked. "I think-"

Jen stared at him. "Now."

He looked at her for a moment before wisely turning and heading back to his friends.

Jen opened the door for Lou. "You okay?"

Lou nodded. She hopped in the car and snapped on her seat belt as Jen got into the driver's side.

Jen glanced over at Lou but Lou looked away. Jen pulled into traffic without a word. Lou watched the world rush by.

A few minutes later, Lou realized they weren't heading for the hotel. She looked over at Jen. "Where are we going?"

"Just up here," Jen said.

Jen made a right and drove through the gates of the Cloverfield cemetery. She headed down the main path before turning down one of the many lanes that branched throughout the cemetery.

Lou looked around in surprise. She knew this place. It was where her Grandma and Mom were buried. Jen pulled over and turned off the engine.

They were both silent for a moment, just looking at the rows and rows of tombstones. Lou recognized the giant angel that sat on the edge of a tombstone three down from her Grandma. They hadn't been able to afford a tombstone that big for either her Mom or Grandma. But Lou had liked to think that the angel was looking out for them as well.

Now as she stared at it, she wasn't sure what to think. Was that one of the good angels or the bad ones? Or was there really any difference? Were they all just bad? Was she bad?

Lou felt the weight in her chest and the burn of tears in the back of her eyes. She turned to Jen. "What are we doing here?"

Jen nodded toward one of the rows. "There's a plot available near your Mom and Grandmother. I arranged to have Charlotte buried there."

Lou glanced over at her in shock. She hadn't even thought about where to bury Charlotte. "Thank you."

Jen nodded.

Lou looked away, taking a shaky breath. "Do they know who did this to her?"

Jen hesitated. "Yes. Sort of."

Lou's head swiveled back. "What do you mean sort of?"

Jen sighed. "It was a Fallen. But I didn't get a look at him."

Lou sat back. "A -" Her mind whirled. "Are you sure?"

"Yes, unfortunately I am."

Lou stared at Jen and then through the windshield at the hovering angel. A Fallen killed Charlotte. The numbness that had settled over her began to burn off as her anger grew. They'd done it. Just like Jen had warned.

"I think it's best if we just get you out of town," Jen said. "I can have you-"

"Wait a minute. What are you talking about?"

"Lou, it's not safe for you. They'll make contact, probably sometime in the next few weeks. They'll wait until you feel really alone and try to recruit you. You need to be long gone."

Lou shook her head. "I'm not going anywhere."

"Lou-"

"They killed Charlotte!" The rage and powerlessness Lou felt came boiling out. "They killed her like she was nothing. They don't get to get away with that."

Jen grabbed her hand. "I *will* get the people that did this. I promise you that. But we need to get you to safety. I can catch them without you."

"How? If I leave, they leave too." An idea began to form in Lou's mind.

"I'll figure something out," Jen said.

"They're doing this to other people. If we don't stop them, other kids like me are going to lose their families as well."

"I know." Jen's words were heavy with understanding. "But that's not your fight."

Lou's eyes cut to Jen. "Yes. It is. And you can use me. Let them recruit me and then you come in with the cavalry."

Jen stared at her for a moment. "Do you have any idea how reckless that is? How dangerous? I won't risk you like that."

Lou looked at Jen, feeling all the loss she had suffered in the last five years. And she was not willing to let anyone else experience the same pain. "It's not your choice. I'm going to find whoever killed Charlotte, with or without your help."

CHAPTER 25

MADDOX WALKED down the long hallway of the hotel, making note of the exits and windows. Jen had picked the top floor and had rented out all the rooms surrounding hers and below hers. That was good.

Jen's brother Jordan had called Maddox and let him know what Lou wanted to do. And he knew Jen was against it. He reached the end of the hall and knocked on the door.

Jen pulled it open with a start. "Maddox? What are you doing here?"

Maddox smiled, noticing the gun behind Jen's back. "Nice to see you too, Jen."

Jen laughed stepping out of the way to let him in, placing the gun in her holster. "Sorry. Come on in. And then tell me what the hell you're doing here."

Maddox stepped in, looking around. "Where's the little angel?"

Jen rolled her eyes. "She's taking a shower. Wait. Who's with Kati and Max?"

"They're with Laney and Jake. They're safe."

"What? I thought we agreed to keep them out of this."

Maddox nodded. "We did and they are. Henry told them what

was going on when they got back. He convinced them to let you two handle it."

Jen took a seat over on the couch. "Okay good. Now, why are *you* here?"

Maddox sat down across from her, his long legs stretched out in front of him. "Well, I hear your new friend is being a little stubborn and wants to go undercover."

Jen blew out a breath. "Who told you?"

"Jordan."

Jen shook her head. "What was he thinking?"

"He was thinking this might be a way to help kids like Lou."

Jen looked away. "Yeah, that's her argument as well."

"Well, if you want my two cents-"

Jen crossed her arms. "I don't."

"- I think it's a good idea."

Jen grit her teeth. "Maddox, she's fifteen years old and just lost her sister. I'm not throwing her into that viper's pit."

Maddox put up his hands. "Hey, I'm not suggesting we leave her there. But she could lead us to them."

"You can't be serious. She's just a kid."

"I'm not saying we send her in as is. We train her. Wait for them to make their move. When they do, we swoop in, grab her, and all the rest."

Jen gave him a long look. "You and I both know it's never that simple."

"No, but it is our current best shot of catching these guys. They're going to keep doing this - going after kids, killing their families to isolate them. Lou can help us end all of that."

Lou stepped into the room in jeans and a t-shirt, her hair wet. "I'm in."

"I thought you were in the shower," Jen said before throwing an annoyed glance at Maddox.

He shrugged.

Lou nodded at Maddox. "I was. But then I felt that tingle that told me we had a guest. I wanted to make sure they were friendly."

Jen glared at Maddox before turning to Lou. "Lou, we don't know when or even if these guys will contact you. You'd have to go into foster care. You could be there for months, maybe even years. This is a long shot."

Maddox glanced at Jen but said nothing. Jen knew they would come for Lou. There'd be no other reason to take out her sister. But he also knew Jen wanted to protect the girl and Maddox couldn't blame her for that.

Lou moved over to them, her arms crossed. "But it's a shot. Without this, it's going to be really hard to find the guys who killed-." She stumbled over the word. Taking a breath, she continued, "- who killed Charlotte. I need to do something."

Even Maddox could see the grief in the girl's eyes. Part of him screamed that this was wrong. This girl was grieving.

But he also knew that if the positions were reversed, he'd want the same thing. He looked at Jen and realized she'd come to the same conclusion.

Jen stared at Lou, forcing the girl to meet her gaze. "On one condition: You train. And if these guys get in touch with you and I don't think you're ready, then I pull the plug."

"Absolutely." Lou smiled, hesitated, and then threw her arms around Jen. "Thanks Jen."

Jen paused for only a moment before returning the hug. And Maddox heard her thoughts as clearly as if she had said them out loud.

Please don't make me regret this.

CHAPTER 26

Henry walked down the hall of the hotel, Danny and Moxy next to him. He knocked at Jen's door.

It was opened a few seconds later by Maddox. "Hey there, boss."

"Hey Maddox." Henry smiled as he walked in followed by Danny.

Maddox resumed his seat on the couch, next to Jordan who gave Henry a distracted wave. Both men were focused on the ballgame on the screen.

Over by the window, Jen sat next to Lou at the dining table. Henry was surprised at how small Lou was. From the way Jen and Maddox had been speaking, he'd expected her to be more intimidating.

Moxy trotted over to Jen, who reached down and rubbed her back. "Hey there Moxy."

Moxy wagged her tail happily before turning to Lou. Lou smiled. "So what is she, a spy dog?"

Jen laughed. "No, just a normal one. This is Moxy."

Lou knelt down. "Who's a good girl?"

Moxy wagged her tail, licking Lou's face. Lou's laugh rang through the room.

A look of concern crossed Jen's face and if he hadn't been watching her so intently Henry probably would have missed it.

Jen walked over to Danny and gave him a hug. "It's good to see you."

Danny hugged her back. "You too."

Jen tugged on his arm. "Come meet Lou."

Danny followed behind her.

"Lou this is Danny," Jen said.

Lou stood up and smiled. "Hi. Jen's told me a lot about you."

"Um, yeah. Nice to meet you." Danny looked down but then almost immediately looked back up and caught Lou's gaze. "I'm sorry about your sister."

Lou's smile dimmed. "Thanks."

Henry stepped forward. "I'm sorry too, Lou. I'm Henry."

Lou's eyes grew bigger as she looked up to his face. "Wow." Her face grew red. "I mean, nice to meet you."

Henry shook her hand. "Jen's told us a lot about you as well."

Lou glanced over at Jen. "Has she told you how much she doesn't want me to do this?"

"Yes," Henry said. "Are you sure you want to?"

Lou nodded, her face tight. "They shouldn't be allowed to get away with this."

Henry watched her for a moment and saw the fear but also the resolve. *Brave kid.*

Danny put the briefcase he carried on the table and snapped it open. He pulled out a small needle shaped object with a small bulge at the end. "Um, I guess we should get started."

Lou leaned forward. "What's that?"

"It's a tracker," Danny said. "We'll insert it in your shoe."

Lou's eyes grew big as she looked from the tracker to Danny. "Cool. Did you design it?"

Danny nodded.

"You're like super smart, right?"

Danny blushed. "Um, sort of."

Lou grinned. "Totally cool."

Danny blushed brighter. Henry tried to hide his grin. He couldn't remember ever seeing Danny interact with a girl his own age.

Jordan walked over and whacked Danny on the shoulder. "Smart? He's smarter than everyone in this room combined."

Lou grinned looking at Maddox who hadn't moved from the couch. "Well, Maddox doesn't really add much to the intelligent quotient."

"True," Jordan agreed.

"You know I can hear you two," Maddox said without turning.

Jordan and Lou looked at each other and then back at Maddox. "We know."

Henry smiled. Jen had mentioned that Jordan and Lou had taken to each other like ducks to water.

"Okay, well, if we're done with the comedy routine," Jen said and Henry could see the tension in her shoulders.

Lou took her seat and held out her hand.

Danny put the tracker in it.

"It's really small. What's the range on it?" Lou asked.

"Fifty miles," Danny said.

"Fifty miles?" Lou swallowed, looking at Jen and then back at Danny. "Um, what happens if you guys don't realize I've been grabbed? Could I go out of range?"

Jen opened her mouth to speak but Maddox cut her off, walking over. "Yes. It's possible - very possible. You'll have a tail at your school, but there are no guarantees. So you need to really think if you want to continue this. You don't need to do this."

"Wait, if I have a tail won't they sense them?" Lou asked.

"Not when I'm your tail," Jordan said.

Lou looked between Jen and Jordan. "Are you another special nephilim, like Laney?"

Henry shook his head. "No. They won't sense him because he's *not* a nephilim. He's a Navy SEAL."

"Wow." Lou looked up at Jen. "You guys are like a totally badass family."

Maddox nodded. "Jordan's good but it doesn't change the fact that there are no guarantees."

Jen nodded. "And you can't fool yourself into thinking there are."

Lou took a deep breath. Holding out her hand, she handed the tracker back to Danny. "They killed Charlotte. I'm in."

CHAPTER 27

TWO DAYS LATER

Lou turned her head on the pillow. The house was quiet. She was pretty sure everyone was asleep.

It was her first night in her foster home. Jen and Jordan had turned her into Children's and Families yesterday after Charlotte's funeral. Lou swallowed hard and let out a shaky breath.

It had been a nice funeral. Jen, Maddox and Jordan had been there. Henry and Danny had even stayed in town to attend. Lou hadn't told anyone at school and none of Charlotte's friends had shown up. But it had been better that way. Henry had even rented the back room of a really fancy Irish pub for a meal afterwards.

But then it had been time to go. She'd spent last night in juvie hall before they'd found a place for her. Lou shuddered. She never wanted to go back there again.

Her foster parents - the Tuttles - weren't bad but their son made her skin crawl. He was twenty-two and built like a truck - a dump truck. That sick feeling crept over her again thinking about his eyes on her at dinner.

Banishing the image, she pictured Jen pulling her aside before they walked into Children's and Families. Jen's eyes had stared straight into Lou's. "You don't have to do this. We can be in Baltimore in a few hours."

Lou had looked at her and felt gratitude. Someone actually cared. And Lou wanted to say yes, let's go.

But then she pictured all the other kids like her who didn't have a Jen in their corner. And here she was.

Lou glanced at the clock on the side table. 1:30 a.m. She'd gone to bed at 10:00 but hadn't been able to sleep.

Her cell buzzed. Lou snatched it from under the pillow, reading the text message from Maddox: Jump out the window and meet me at the end of the block.

Lou stared at it for a moment in disbelief, before typing a reply. I'm on the third floor.

Maddox's reply was quick in coming: I know. Jump out the window and meet me at the end of the block. Don't forget to roll when you hit the ground. Training begins now.

Lou sat up and slid her feet into her sneakers. *Jump out the window?*

She walked to the window that overlooked the back yard. The yard looked really far away.

Hitching up the window, she threw one leg over and looked down. *This is not crazy,* she told herself as she threw over her other leg.

Grabbing onto the ledge, she lowered herself over, holding on only by her fingertips. She let out a breath. *Well, here goes nothing.*

She let go. Time seemed to stop. She fell in what seemed to be minutes. As she neared the ground, she tucked. Rolling as she hit, she bounced up to her feet.

She stood still, her jaw gaping as she looked up at her window. Then a grin spread across her face. *I just did that.* She nearly let out a laugh but covered her mouth. *Holy crap.*

With a skip in her step, she vaulted the back fence and ran down the block. An Explorer sat idling at the curb. A tingle ran through her.

Lou picked up her pace and opened the door to see Jordan

sitting in the back seat with Jen and Maddox upfront. She grinned. "Hi guys."

Jordan frowned at her.

Maddox barked at her from the driver's seat. "Next time, make sure we're the good guys before you blindly open a door."

Her smile slipped a little. "Uh yeah. Sorry."

Jen looked over her shoulder at her from the passenger seat, an eyebrow raised. "Welcome to your first day of training."

CHAPTER 28

They trained every night for three hours for two weeks. They kept the training simple: basic self defense moves and avoidance strategies. And Jen had to admit that Lou was a natural. She seemed to be able to almost sense what she or Maddox was going to do before they did it.

Henry had even come down to try his skill on her. She'd done pretty well. But Jen wasn't ready to sign off. Not yet.

"Everything ready?" Maddox asked Jen as he walked into the old manufacturing plant with Lou. The plant had been abandoned two decades ago due to financial problems. And no one had been interested in buying the place since then.

Jen smiled. "Yup."

Lou curled a bicep. "Well, bring it on."

"Oh, I see we're getting a little cocky," Maddox said.

Lou grinned. "Not cocky. Just confident."

"Well, we'll see how you do after tonight." Jen pointed to the path behind her that led between the giant machines. "Head down that way until you see a catwalk overhead. When you're under it, we begin. Same rules: find and capture."

"Yes, ma'am." Lou gave Jen a salute before she headed down the path with a skip in her step.

Jen crossed her arms watching Lou disappear, trying hard not to smile. She was really beginning to like this kid.

Maddox stood next to her. "The surprise in place?"

Jen nodded. "Yup."

"Think she's ready?"

Jen smiled up at him. "Nope."

CHAPTER 29

Lou walked down the path following its twists and turns. The plant was dark. Although she was feeling more confident in her skills, the place did leave her feeling a little creeped out.

Up ahead, she saw the catwalk. "Let the games begin," she whispered as she reached it.

Lou went still, listening to see if she could sense or hear anyone. Nothing. Lou moved forward slowly, sticking to the shadows.

A creak sounded from the catwalk above her, but she didn't sense anyone. She grinned. *Hello Jordan.*

Lou ran down the path. She leaped on top of a conveyor belt before jumping for the catwalk. Landing lightly in a crouch, she peered ahead and saw movement. She grinned. He was making this way too easy.

She sprinted down the catwalk. A shadow disappeared right at the end with a flash of blonde hair.

Gotcha. She ran for the movement and stopped. The catwalk dead-ended in an empty space, heavy with shadows. *What the hell?*

She spun hearing a clink of metal from below. "How the hell did you get down there so fast?" she murmured.

One arm on the railing, she jumped over the side. She landed in a roll and bounced to her feet.

A noise sounded to her left. Lou ran quickly along the path when a noise from her right pulled her to a stop. *How did he get over there?*

She chased noises for ten minutes - occasionally catching a glimpse of Jordan dressed all in black. But every time she thought she had him, he disappeared and reappeared across the factory.

Now she stood under the catwalk where she'd first started. Frustration rolled through her. This should be easier. Jordan was human - he didn't have her skills. How was he staying out of her grasp?

She couldn't hear anything and the machines towered above her, making it hard to see. Lou leapt to the top of one and jumped from container to container. She crouched down low and scanned the room.

Where was he? For a human, he moved really fast.

Up ahead she heard a movement, as if someone had stepped on a grate. She smiled. *Got you now.*

Moving silently, she climbed down the machine, making her way to the spot where she'd heard the noise. If she was right, he was over near the giant turbine. Another creak of metal had her moving faster. She smiled.

Hunched over, she made her way quickly down the path. She stopped at the end of the aisle. Hidden by the machine, she paused, straining to hear. Nothing. But then, a scuffle sounded. She peeked out. He was twenty feet away, his back to her.

She stepped out ready to sprint over and take him down. But a piece of metal tapped her on the back. "You're dead," whispered a voice.

The man behind her grabbed her by the shoulder and turned her around.

She stared at him in disbelief. "What the hell?"

CHAPTER 30

"That was completely unfair," Lou yelled.

Jen crossed her arms over her chest. "How was that unfair?"

Lou spluttered. "They're - they're - they're twins."

Jen raised an eyebrow, nodding to where her brothers sat drinking some water. They saluted her with their water bottles. "Were you not aware of the existence of twins in the world?"

Lou ran her hands through her hair, looking like she wanted to yank some of it out. "Of course I know twins exist. But first you give me humans, and then you give me identical humans. It wasn't a fair test."

"Why not?"

"Because I wasn't ready. I wasn't expecting that."

Jen used her height to tower over Lou. "Exactly. You weren't ready and you got sloppy. You saw your target and you didn't think there might be another danger."

"But, I mean, what the hell's the chance I'm going to go against identical twins?"

"I don't know, Lou. What's the chance you're going to go against lab created gigantic leopards? Because you know what, that's what my friends faced when they went up against these guys."

Lou reared back. "What? You're kidding, right?"

"No, I'm not." Jen was relieved to see fear cross Lou's face. Lou had been taking this all way too lightly. "You need to understand what you might be up against. You are never safe. You can never let your guard down. You can never be cocky. You think this was unfair? Just wait. You haven't even begun to see unfair."

Jordan walked over. "Lou, you've been doing really well with training. But Jen's right. You need to always be on guard. You can't be so focused on the prize that you forget about the threats - even when the prize is within reach. Actually, *especially* when the prize is within reach. That's when you need to be even more vigilant."

Lou sighed, her shoulders slumped. "I know you guys are right. It's just . . . I don't know." She scuffed her shoe along the floor.

Jen put a hand on her shoulder. "It's just you thought you were doing well. And now you feel like you're not. You *have* been doing well. But my brothers here, well they've been doing this for years. You've had weeks."

Jordan nodded. "And even then, I could have sworn you had me back at the catwalk. It was really close."

"How did you get away?" Lou asked.

Jordan grinned. "I dropped into a corner of shadows, pulled my hood over my head, and held my breath. You walked right by me."

"Seriously?" Lou grouched. "That's how I missed you?"

Jordan shrugged. "Sometimes hiding in plain sight works. You were expecting me to keep moving, so I decided to stop moving. If you're in a tight spot and your enemy expects you to do one thing, do the opposite."

Lou nodded. "Yeah, okay."

Maddox put an arm around her. "You're doing good, kid. But this is just a reminder: the bad guys don't play fair. So don't expect them to."

Lou nodded.

Jen watched her - still not sure this was the right thing. Lou had been doing well but she was just a kid. She wasn't ready for this.

Jen also knew that part of Lou was latching onto the idea of finding Charlotte's killer as a way to avoid dealing with Charlotte's death.

Lou glanced at Jen. In the dim light, she looked so young.

Jordan tapped Jen on the shoulder and gave a barely perceptible shake of his head. He knew Jen wanted to try and talk her out of it again.

She sighed. *God I hate this.*

Lou looked up. A smile returned to her face. "Okay. Let's go again. Best two out of three?"

Jordan nodded. "I'm game."

"Me too," Mike said as he walked up.

They all looked to Jen. But Jen kept her eyes on Lou.

"I've got this," Lou said.

Jen knew Lou was talking about more than the exercise. She nodded. "Okay. Let's go again."

CHAPTER 31

Two nights later, Henry stretched out on the couch in his home office. He'd made another trip to Detroit. Ostensibly the trip had been so Danny could check the tracker. But Henry knew he could have had someone else do that. He had wanted to see that Jen was okay.

And she was for the most part. But he knew it didn't sit well with her to string Lou out as bait, even if Lou was the one who'd put herself on the hook. He couldn't blame her.

But from what little he knew about Lou, he could tell she was committed. If they didn't help her, she'd try to go after them herself.

He shook his head, trying to focus on the papers in his hand. He should be looking over the contract with the Venezuelan group that he was supposed to sign.

He placed them on the coffee table next to him after reading and re-reading the opening paragraphs a few times. He closed his eyes. *Five minutes and I'll get right back to them.*

Danny shook his shoulder a while later waking him. "Um, Henry?"

Henry looked at Danny and then wiped his eyes sitting up. "Hey Danny. What time is it?"

"Close to midnight."

Henry rubbed his face. "I must have fallen asleep. What are you up to?"

Henry noticed for the first time how pale Danny was. He scooted over on the couch and gestured for Danny to take a seat.

Danny did - a file in his hand.

"What's wrong?" Henry asked.

Danny handed him a folder. "I found something out."

Henry took the folder but kept his eyes on Danny. Danny stayed quiet, so Henry opened it. Inside were police reports on four separate homicides in the last six months and a list of the teenagers they'd liberated from the second camp. Four names were highlighted.

Henry looked up. "I don't get it. What is this?"

Danny swallowed. "I'm not entirely sure. But it seems that at the same time some of those guys were recruited, there were murders in their neighborhoods."

"Okay, horrible but that happens. Some of these kids are from some really violent areas."

Danny nodded. "I know but look at how the victims were killed."

Henry scanned the reports. All the victims were middle-aged women. They had been found sitting in a chair in their living room - even though none of them had been killed in the chair - with their throats cut and dozens of stab wounds.

Henry stared at Danny and he saw the eight-year old boy he'd met seven years ago. Without Danny saying a word, Henry had known how unhappy he was, how rough he was having it at home.

Once Henry had gotten to know Danny, he'd promised himself he would give Danny a safe home - a place where violence wouldn't touch him.

Henry stared at the reports in front of him. And now the boy he'd promised himself he would protect from danger was showing him evidence of a serial killer at work.

He cleared his throat. "I'm sure it's just a coincidence."

"A coincidence? Henry, these murders all happened in different states. But they all happened when someone was recruiting. Statistically, the likelihood that these are not related is nonexistent."

Henry sighed, knowing fighting Danny on facts was an effort in futility. "I know. I know."

Danny bit his lip.

A feeling of dread pooled in Henry's stomach. "Is there more?"

"Yeah. The last murder in that file was after we raided the last camp. Which means the killer is still out there." Danny handed Henry another sheet of paper. "And this is a homicide on the same night that Lou's sister was killed."

Henry took the sheet knowing what he was going to find. Catherine Pearce, age fifty-four, had been found in her living room with her throat cut and over a dozen stab wounds to her chest.

He looked up at Danny as dread spread through him.

Danny nodded. "I think you should call Jen."

CHAPTER 32

JEN PACED the living room floor of the suite. "She's okay," Maddox said from the couch.

Jen nodded but kept pacing. "I know."

Jordan had called a few minutes ago to say he'd picked up Lou and was on the way. And Jen trusted Jordan. She knew hell or high water he'd keep her safe. But still, Henry's news had scared the hell out of her and she'd been on edge ever since.

A knock sounded at the door halting her ruminations.

"See? There she is." Maddox crossed the room and opened the door.

"You're sure this is safe?" Lou asked as she walked in, Jordan behind her.

"Yes. Come on in. Breakfast is already here." Jen studied Lou. There were some dark circles under her eyes, but overall she looked good. Her clothes were clean and there was an energy around her.

"I'll be down the hall if you need me." Jordan pulled the door closed. Jen knew he was going to be by the elevator, making sure no one entered the floor. There were also two other Chandler operatives stationed at the hotel.

"Hey kid," Maddox said.

"Hey coach," Lou answered heading straight for the table and taking a seat. "Man this looks good."

Jen sat down across from her. "Aren't they feeding you over there?"

Lou nodded, picking up her fork. "They are. I'm just really hungry lately."

Maddox took a seat at the table and picked up his fork. "It's your abilities. It's like a growth spurt. You're burning off calories faster than you can replace them right now. It'll slow up in a few years."

Lou nodded. "Hey fine by me."

Maddox looked at Jen and nudged his head toward Lou.

Jen shook her head.

Lou looked between the two of them. "So what's up?"

"What do you mean?" Jen said, stalling.

Lou gave a little laugh. "You know I know you guys at this point, right?" She pointed her fork at Maddox. "Maddox here looks like he wants to tell me something and you look like you're going to throw him out of the window if he says anything."

"Actually, it was going to be through the wall," Jen mumbled.

Lou stabbed at her pancakes. "Ha - I knew it. So spill."

Jen sighed, knowing she had lost this battle. "Okay. I got a call from Henry last night." Jen explained about the women who had been killed so far and their connection to the recruits.

Lou's appetite seemed to diminish with every word Jen said. Finally, she pushed her plate away. "Man, those poor women."

Jen nodded. "Now we need to decide if we pull you out because-"

Lou jerked her head back up. "Wait, pull me out? Why?"

"Didn't you just hear what I said? Someone's killing people while recruiting," Jen said.

Lou shook her head. "Yeah but they're not killing nephilim or Fallen. In fact, whoever is killing them seems to have a specific type - a type which is not me."

"True," Maddox said.

Jen glared at him.

"Which means I'm not in danger," Lou continued. "Other people are. So I'm not getting what's changed."

Jen shook her head. "We don't know that for sure. All we know is that these murders and the recruitment are connected. It's not safe."

Lou let out a laugh but there was no joy in it. "Safe? Do you know what my life was like before all of this? I lived in one of the worst neighborhoods ever. Crossing a war zone was safer than walking to school. My mom was killed. My sister was killed. I'm only here because of my freaky abilities or I would have died that night in the park. I've never been safe."

"But you can be safe now. We can keep you safe," Jen said.

Lou shook her head. "And what about the other kids, huh? The other ones like me who get targeted and don't have you backing them up? Who's going to keep them safe?" Lou looked at Maddox. "You agree with me. I know you do."

Maddox held Lou's gaze for a moment and then turned to Jen. "I do. The guy who's targeting these people, he's not going to stop just because Lou gets tucked away. If we're lucky, we can catch him as well as find the training camp."

"See?" Lou said. "This is the best course of action. And before you say anything, I *know* it's dangerous but I *choose* to do this. I choose to help."

Jen wanted to strangle her and at the same time she was so proud she could burst. "Lou, I can't ask you -"

Lou cut her off. "You're not asking me to do anything. I'm telling you that I'm staying here. I'm doing this. You try to take me away and I'll just run."

Jen looked at Lou who met her gaze without blinking. She had to admit, the girl had courage. But Jen couldn't help but feel responsible. She never should have mentioned anything about this killer. It only seemed to increase Lou's resolve.

"Jen, I want to do this. I need to do this," Lou said.

"Lou, these people - " Jen shook her head trying to figure out a way to convey in a few words just how dangerous they truly were. "They're just- they're evil, Lou. I don't want you around that."

"Well, you're not my mom. She's dead. Just like my grandma and my sister. I couldn't do anything about my mom and grandma but at least I can catch the guy who took Charlotte."

Jen sighed, knowing she'd lost. "Two more weeks. If these guys don't make a move by then, we're gone. Okay?"

Lou nodded. "Okay."

CHAPTER 33

A WEEK AND A HALF LATER, Lou was worried. Not because someone might contact her - but because they might not.

She knew Jen would keep her word and pull her at the end of the week. She was annoyed at Jen but at the same time, it was nice having someone worry about her for a change.

Lou glanced around the athletic fields as she headed for the bleachers. Even though she was at a different school, her life was still the same. Actually, if she was being honest, it was a little easier. She didn't have to worry about rent. And while the Tuttle's weren't exactly warm and fuzzy, she always had clean clothes and food.

The high school itself was better. I mean, it wasn't what you saw on TV with the shiny lockers and pristine football field. But it was definitely a step up from her last one. The history books even went up to 2010. Still out of date, but a heck of a lot closer.

Lou climbed the bleacher stairs. Taking a seat two rows from the top, she pulled the brown lunch bag Mrs. Glover had packed from her backpack. Looking inside, she shook her head - peanut butter and jelly again.

With a sigh, she unwrapped the sandwich. *Would it kill her to change things up a bit? Maybe a turkey sandwich? I'd even take tuna fish.*

Lou took a bite and went still as a thin shot of electricity ran through her. Heart pounding, she reminded herself to keep calm.

Jen's instructions rolled through her mind. *Just because you can feel them, doesn't mean they can feel you. If it's a nephilim, they won't feel anything. If it's a Fallen, no need to clue them in that you realize who they are.*

Grabbing her water bottle, Lou couldn't help but notice the shake in her hand. She took a drink and stared at the field where a gym class was running track.

She forced herself to not look around. But her senses were on high alert for any sign of someone moving in.

She waited a few seconds but nothing happened. Nothing changed.

Keeping her movements unhurried, she reached into her bag. Her hand curled around her phone.

The feeling appeared again. A boy stood at the bottom of the stairs. He was short, not even five feet. Honestly, he didn't look old enough to be in high school. *It couldn't be him, could it?*

He smiled but Lou cut her gaze away.

Undeterred he walked up the stairs and sat next to her. "Hi Lou."

Lou had never seen him before but everything in her screamed that he was a Fallen. She put an edge to her voice. "Do I *know* you?"

"Nope. But we're going to be good friends. I'm Pascha."

Lou grabbed her backpack and stood. "Yeah, well, *Pascha*, I don't need any more friends."

He moved to block her way.

Lou glared down at him. "Look, kid, I don't know you. So get out of my way."

His face went hard. "I'm not a kid."

She stepped down to the next row of seats. "Whatever."

From the corner of her eye, she saw him reach out to grab her arm. She twisted out of the way lightning fast, shoving him with her other hand.

He laughed as he fell back landing in a crouch. He straightened with a grin. "So you do have your powers. I was beginning to wonder. Look, I've been sent to tell you there's a place for you."

"A place for me? What the hell are you talking about?"

He watched her for a moment. "You're special like me. You know that, don't you?"

Lou watched him for a moment debating what to do. Maddox's advice sounded in her mind. *Be interested but not too interested. After all, you're supposed to be a bit of a hard case.*

"Yeah. What of it?" Lou asked.

"Well, there's a place where you can learn more about your abilities - how to use them. And you'll meet others like you."

Lou watched him but said nothing. Pascha seemed to take it as interest.

"I know you're in foster care," he continued. "You lost your sister. It's got to be rough."

He looked at her with what she knew was supposed to be a comforting look. But it needed practice.

And behind his mouth, there was the glimmer of a smirk. Lou knew as soon as that smirk appeared that this was the monster who'd killed Charlotte. She dug her fingers into her palms to keep her hands from reaching for his neck.

"I'm like you. And there are others like us." He gestured toward the kids running on the track. "We don't have to be like these sheep."

Lou scoffed. "Okay, let's say I believe you. What do you want besides to introduce me to people like me? You just thinking we should all be friends?"

He stood up with a laugh. "Hardly. I think you know no one just helps people without getting something in return. And the people I work for want something, but it'll be something you want to give."

"Yeah, see I'm not a big fan of not knowing what I'm getting into." Lou turned to walk away, hoping she was making the right move.

She got only a few feet before Pascha's voice stopped her.

"There's money. Lots of it."

Lou turned around. "What do you mean?"

"I mean money. More than you'll ever get with some measly job around here. Why not come try it out? What have you got to lose?"

Lou watched him for a moment, knowing that if she hadn't met Jen, this pitch would be really tempting. And right now, she needed to act like she hadn't met Jen. She crossed her arms over her chest. "Okay. Let's say I want to know more."

Pascha smiled. "Then I'd say you were making the smart choice. Besides, you have a better offer?"

Lou looked him in the eye, thinking of Charlotte and Jen - and she imagined killing the boy in front of her.

Slowly, she shook her head. "No. I guess I don't."

CHAPTER 34

PASCHA STARTED to head down the bleacher stairs. "Well, come on."

"What? Now?" Lou asked.

"Why not? You don't have any ties - no one to say good-bye to. Why wait?"

Lou scrambled for a way to stall him. "Um, but I don't have my clothes, my toothbrush, anything."

Pascha waved away her concerns as they reached the bottom of the steps. He headed toward the gate that led to the parking lot. "Don't worry about any of that. We'll get you all new stuff when we get there."

"Um, okay. Cool." Lou followed him out into the parking lot. Slowly, she reached into her bag.

He turned suddenly. "Oh hey, do you have a phone?"

Lou nodded. "Yeah, why?"

He held out his hand. "Can I see it?"

Lou pulled it out and handed it over. "Uh, yeah sure. You need to make a call?"

Pascha just smiled, then he threw the phone to the ground and stomped on it.

"What the hell?" Lou yelled.

Pascha shrugged. "Your foster parents will probably report you missing. We don't want them tracking you through the phone. Don't worry. We'll give you one of those as well."

Lou stared at him and then at the broken pieces of her phone scattered across the ground. How the hell was she going to tell Jen what was going on?

He stared at her. "What's wrong?"

Angry, you'd be angry not scared, she reminded herself. She gritted her teeth. "That was my phone. And you could have just turned *off* the GPS."

Shrugging, he turned and walked through the gate to the parking lot. "Yeah. But like I said, we'll get you a new one. Money's not an issue."

Lou stared after him. If she didn't go with him now, there was a chance they'd lose him entirely. He might never contact her again. *Damn.* She ran after him.

"You drive?" Lou asked as she caught up with him. He couldn't be more than twelve.

"No need," he said as a limo pulled up to the curb. He looked at Lou expectantly.

"Cool," she said feigning enthusiasm. He seemed to buy it. As the limo stopped, the driver got out and opened the back door. Pascha gestured for Lou to go ahead of him.

Lou climbed into the back and slid along the black leather seats. Pascha followed her in. A few seconds after the door closed, they took off. Lou struggled not to stare out the window looking for Jordan.

Instead, she sat in the back, watching the world she had known her whole life slip past her until she didn't recognize where they were any more. She turned to Pascha. "Where are we going?"

"For a little ride." He gestured to the sign up ahead.

Lou's heart almost stopped - Detroit Metropolitan Airport.

A plane. Why didn't we think of a plane?

She thought of the tracker in her shoe. It was only good for fifty miles and Jen, Jordan and Maddox didn't even know she was on the move.

She swallowed hard. She was on her own.

CHAPTER 35

JEN PACED along the floor in the suite. She was probably going to have to pay to have the carpet replaced if this went on much longer.

Maddox lay sprawled on the couch. "Jen, you need to relax."

"Can't," she said and left it at that.

She pushed back the curtains and stared out the window. She hated being cooped up in here when Lou could be in trouble. No one had made any moves on her yet. But from Jen's perspective that meant each day increased the likelihood that this would be the day.

She would have felt better if she and Maddox were watching her at the school. Actually, she'd feel better if they were on a plane back to Baltimore with Lou.

Until that time, though, she and Maddox were holed up in the hotel. They knew a Fallen or a nephilim would most likely be the one who made contact. And they didn't want to take the chance that he or she would sense Jen or Maddox. So, they couldn't go anywhere near the school.

Jen pulled out her phone but Lou hadn't checked in. She normally called during her lunch break.

Probably nothing, Jen thought. But she couldn't shake the feeling that something was off.

Her phone rang and Jen looked at the screen. Jordan. Dread pierced through her. She clicked on the phone. "What's wrong?"

"They made contact," Jordan yelled and Jen could tell he was driving. "She's on the move."

"On the move? Where?" Jen was already running for the door, Maddox on her heels. Together they raced down the hall. By mutual silent agreement, they skipped the elevator and started sprinting down the stairs.

"The airport."

"What?" Fear coursed through her. "Jordan, that tracker's only good for fifty miles. If she gets on a plane-" Jen couldn't finish the sentence. The idea was too unbearable.

"I know," Jordan said quietly. "We'll lose her."

CHAPTER 36

Lou walked down the Jetway toward the plane, trying not to act as terrified as she felt. Pascha had given her a fake ID and a plane ticket. Beside her, he nudged her arm. "Ever flown before?"

"Um no."

"Well, don't worry. It's perfectly safe."

She nodded, not sure what to say. But if he thought she was terrified of a little plane flight, so much the better.

She followed Pascha down the plane aisle and into their seats. Pascha took the window seat without asking if she wanted it. But being she already thought he was a slimy piece of crap, it didn't really reduce her opinion of him.

Lou stuffed the magazines she'd picked up in the seat pocket in front of her. Belting herself in, she drummed her fingers on the hand rest.

I'm sitting next to the person who killed Charlotte. She glanced over at Pascha and imagined bashing his head against the wall of the plane.

But if you do that, you lose your chance at helping find the others like you. Lou looked away with effort.

"Still nervous?" Pasha asked.

"Um, yeah, well, you know. First time and all," Lou answered staring straight ahead.

"Well, it'll be fine." Pasha put on his headphones, closed his eyes and turned to the window.

Lou stared at him in disbelief. *Gee thanks for the heartfelt pep talk.*

Lou looked around. There was a family across from her - Mom, Dad, and a little girl. The girl smiled at her. Lou smiled back before turning away.

Lou looked past Pasha's sleeping form to the sky outside. A plane. They would never be able to track her on a plane. What the hell had she been thinking? She was in way over her head.

Someone bumped into her chair. "Oh sorry."

Lou looked up into Jordan's eyes and had to keep from crying out in relief.

She just nodded. "It's okay."

Jordan continued on to his seat. Lou forced herself to not look for where he was. He was here. They knew where she was. She wasn't alone.

She let out a breath. *Okay. I can do this.*

CHAPTER 37

Jen sat in the passenger seat of Maddox's SUV. Maddox skirted around a city bus, barely missing the bumper. Jen didn't even blink.

Jordan had just called and told them he'd gotten on the same flight as Lou. Some of the fear that had filled Jen with Jordan's first call dissipated. As soon as she disconnected the call with him, she called Henry. He picked up immediately. "Hi Jen."

"They have her. She's on a commercial flight to Boston. Jordan's on the same flight."

"Got it. I'll call you back." Henry hung up without another word.

Maddox took the turn into the private airfield almost on two wheels. The Chandler jet sat idling on the tarmac. Henry had left it for them in case of emergency. Jen and Maddox were out of the car as soon as it stopped and up the steps into the plane a few seconds later.

Maddox disappeared into the cockpit while Jen sat down, buckling herself in.

Her phone rang and Jen snatched it up. "Henry?"

"I've arranged for operatives to meet Jordan and I contacted the SIA. They're sending agents as well."

Jen leaned back against the seat closing her eyes. "That's good. We should be there a little before they land."

"I'll have a car waiting for you two. But let the operatives take the lead. They'll be human. The Fallen won't be able to sense them."

Jen bit her lip. She knew that was smart. But she wanted to rush in and grab Lou. She didn't want her spending any more time with these people than necessary. "Who are you sending?"

"About a dozen operatives and Yoni."

Jen felt the tightness in her chest ease a little more. Yoni Benjamin was the five foot two former Navy SEAL and Israeli army officer who worked for the Chandler Group. He was also one of the few people she trusted with Lou. "Good. And make sure we have enough receivers for Lou's tracker."

"Yes, ma'am."

Jen groaned. "Sorry. Thank you - for everything."

"We'll get her back Jen. And we'll get the rest of the kids too."

Jen nodded. "I know."

"Do you?"

She sighed. "No. But I hope so."

CHAPTER 38

BOSTON, MASSACHUSETTS

Jordan hadn't said a word to Lou or even looked at her the whole flight. She'd made eye contact with him when she'd taken a trip to the bathroom. But that had been it.

Knowing he was here, though, calmed her considerably.

When they disembarked, she had to force herself not to look for him. Instead, she kept her eyes straight ahead, trusting Jordan to follow.

Pascha led her through the airport. He bypassed the baggage claim and headed straight for the curb.

Lou stepped out of the airport following him. The noise of planes and traffic assaulted her.

From the corner of her eye, Lou saw Jordan wave at a car which pulled up to the curb. A short bald man Lou didn't recognize sat at the wheel. Without a glance at her, Jordan got into the passenger seat and the car pulled away.

But Lou knew that Jen and Maddox had to be around here somewhere, even though she couldn't sense them. They would stay out of range to make sure Pascha didn't pick up on them either.

They knew where she was. They'd come get her. She had to have faith in that.

"Ready?" Pascha asked as he came to stand next to her.

Lou nodded. "Um, yeah. Where are we going anyway?"

Pascha smiled. "To meet everyone. And this time I got to choose the location. You're going to love it."

"Uh sure. Are we getting a taxi?"

Pascha laughed pointing down the way. "Of course not. That's our ride."

A white van pulled up toward them. Lou was surprised to see a couple of other teenagers already in the back. Lou felt the electric tingles roll over her. Not everyone in the van had powers though.

Pascha took the passenger seat leaving Lou to struggle with the panel door. She climbed in and slid it closed behind her. Then she had to climb to the back row, because all the other seats were taken.

No one smiled at her and a few straight up glared. *Oh, well glad I'm risking my neck for such a nice group of people.*

She took a seat. Sitting next to her was a guy about her age with mocha colored skin and light green eyes. He nodded at her and she nodded back.

Twenty minutes into the drive, Lou was looking anxiously out the window and drumming her hand on her thighs. *Where was the cavalry? Shouldn't they be here already?*

Lou bit her lip. Maybe they were waiting until they got to where ever they were going.

Another fifteen minutes passed in silence. Then the guy next to her leaned his head closer to her. "Hey, um, you doing okay?"

Lou looked over at him. "Yeah. I'm good."

"Awesome because I'm freaking out."

Lou gave a little laugh. "Well, we signed up for this."

He glanced out the window, a nervous smile on his face. "Actually, I'm not really sure what I signed up for. I was kind of thinking of this as summer camp for people with superpowers." He nudged his chin toward the driver and Pascha before leaning down to Lou. "But those two are not the happy counselors I had in mind."

Lou laughed quietly, feeling relief that at least someone here seemed normal. "Yeah I know what you mean. My name's Lou by the way." She held out her hand.

He shook it. "Rolly."

"Rolly? Seriously?"

"It's really Ronald." He rolled his eyes. "My little sister couldn't pronounce it so she started calling me Rolly. It just sort of stuck."

"Is she here?"

He gave her a surprised look. "No. Why would she be here?"

Lou scrambled for an answer. She wasn't supposed to know anything other than what she'd been told by Pascha. God, barely into this spy stuff and already she was blowing her cover. "Um, I just thought maybe they brought both of you."

"Nah. She's my half-sister. After my Mom died, she went to live with her Dad. I went to live with mine." A shadow of grief flickered across Rolly's face.

"Sorry."

He shrugged. "Just the way it goes. Anyway, do you have any idea where we're heading?"

"I'm guessing here." Lou looked out the window as the van turned onto the rest area ramp. Two men pulled back the sawhorses that blocked the way and replaced them after the van was through. Lou didn't feel anything as they passed. The men must be humans.

The van driver pulled into a spot right next to the bathrooms.

Pascha looked back at everyone in the van. "Everybody out."

Lou glanced at Rolly who shrugged back. Then she followed the rest of the teenagers out of the van. There were eight teenagers in total including her and Rolly.

The driver went to the back of the van and pulled out a big canvas bag. He carried it to Pascha. After dropping it to the ground, he unzipped it and started pulling plastic wrapped parcels out of it.

Pascha took a handful of packages. He glanced at the first one and called out. "Derek Bier."

A beefy guy with dark hair stepped forward. "Um here."

Pascha tossed the bag at him. The driver and Pascha then called out everyone else's name. Lou caught her bag and looked inside. It contained a black tracksuit, a t-shirt, socks, sneakers, a sports bra and underwear.

She glanced at the tags. *How'd they get my sizes?*

"All right," Pascha called out pulling everyone's attention. "Each of you will head inside, get changed into these clothes, and put your old stuff into the bag. *All* your old stuff."

"Um why?" one of the guys asked.

Pascha's eyes narrowed at him. Lou held her breath. But finally Pascha smiled. "You are starting a new chapter of your life. You need to do that by leaving your old life behind."

Everyone glanced at one another.

Pascha waved them toward the building. "Go on. You have five minutes."

Lou walked behind Rolly, her mind racing. Maybe she could extract the tracker and place it in her new shoes.

Lou tried to keep from running. She did speed walk a little though and managed to be the first one into the rest room. She grabbed the first stall and quickly changed clothes. Then she sat on the toilet, trying to fish the tracker out of her sneakers.

"Come on, come on," she whispered, but the tracker was buried too deep.

What the hell was she going to do? Without the tracker, Jen wouldn't be able to find her.

Pascha's voice came through the rest room. "Time's up, ladies."

Heart racing, Lou looked down at her old sneaker. *What do I do?*

CHAPTER 39

The recruits lined up outside the van. The driver appeared from the back of the van with a wand of some sort. He started to walk down the line, waving it over each person.

"Uh, what's this?" Rolly asked.

Pascha stepped forward. "Glad you asked. There's a group that's been trying to thwart our efforts - keep you from fulfilling your true potential. We're just making sure that none of you are in league with them."

Lou tried to keep her face impassive, but she could feel her heart hammering through her chest as the driver made his way down the line. Finally, the driver walked up and waved the wand over her. No beeps sounded and she let out a breath. The driver gave her a curious look but she just shrugged.

He moved on to Rolly, who was last in line.

Then the driver went over to the pile of bags. Lou tried to look nonchalant. He ran the wand over each bag.

No beeps sounded.

At the last minute Lou had dumped her shoes in the garbage bin in the bathroom. She didn't even know why she did it, but right now she was glad she did.

The driver stepped away from the pile and nodded at Pascha.

Pascha turned back to them. "Excellent. You all passed. Back in the van."

Lou's legs felt wobbly as she looked around. *Jen, where are you?*

CHAPTER 40

Jen barreled down the highway. Henry sat in the passenger seat, flinching as Jen barely avoided clipping a Toyota. A sharp intake of breath, though, was all the protest he made.

Henry had met Jen and Maddox at the airport. Jen didn't even pretend she wasn't happy to see him.

They'd been following Lou's tracker but staying back out of range. Jordan was ahead with Yoni and the other fully human agents.

"Anything?" Jen asked.

"Not yet," Henry replied.

Ten minutes ago, they realized Lou's tracker hadn't moved. Jen white knuckled the steering wheel. That meant they had either arrived at their destination or -

Jen shied away from that thought. She wasn't going down that road. Not yet.

Jordan and Yoni were doing recon on the site before they entered.

Jordan's voice rang out through the car. "Jordan for Henry."

Henry grabbed the radio. "Go ahead Jordan."

"You guys can come up. There's no one here."

"What?" Jen exclaimed even as she pressed the gas pedal down farther.

She shot up the rest area ramp and pulled to an abrupt stop. Throwing the car into park, she vaulted out of it.

Jordan jogged up, his face tight. "The trackers still here. But Lou's not. No one is."

Yoni stepped out of the rest room area, something in his hands. Jen squinted, trying to see what he held. Then she went still as she recognized the object in Yoni's hand. "Those are Lou's shoes."

Yoni nodded as he stopped in front of her. "Tracker's still in them."

Jen looked up the road, feeling her stomach bottom out. "Oh my God. We lost her."

CHAPTER 41

JEN WALKED AWAY from the group at the rest stop. She needed a few moments alone. Jordan and Yoni were sending people down the highway. They'd cover as much distance as they could. Henry had birds in the air as well but the van could be anywhere.

Henry had called Danny to pull in any footage from the highway and the surrounding areas. But this rescue had just become a giant search.

Jen's stomach clenched painfully. *And if they switched cars, we'll never find them.*

She wrapped her arms around herself. *I never should have let her go. I should have made her go to Baltimore, even if she hated me for it.*

Fear crawled up her throat threatening to choke her. What if Lou got hurt? What if she got killed?

"Jen?"

Jen whirled around as Henry walked up behind her.

He stepped within an arm's reach. "We've notified every law enforcement agency in the area to look out for the van. I've also put a BOLO out on Lou. And Danny's tracking the data as fast as he can."

Jen nodded, knowing that everyone was doing everything they could. And also knowing that it might not be enough.

"We'll find her."

Jen shook her head. "You know the chances of that are getting slimmer by the minute. I never should have let her go. I should have forced her to stay or I should have sent her to the school in Baltimore. This is all my fault."

"It's not your fault. She chose this. I know how hard you tried to keep her from it."

Jen looked away from Henry's knowing eyes. "What if we're too late?"

Henry stepped toward her, wrapping his arms around her. She leaned her head against his chest. Henry's voice was confident. "We won't be."

But Jen didn't share his confidence because there was no room for confidence in her.

Right now, there was only room for mind numbing fear.

CHAPTER 42

Lou and Rolly were once again in the last row of the van. And yet again, silence dominated. As the miles stretched by, though, people began to make small talk. Up front, Pascha tuned into a local radio station and music filled the van.

Rolly leaned down to Lou. "That was kind of weird, right?"

Lou nodded staring out the window looking for a face she recognized in the passing cars. "Yeah. It was."

Rolly looked down at his tracksuit. "This all has a kind of 'welcome to the cult' vibe, doesn't it?"

"Yeah."

Rolly sighed, pulling the jacket a little away from him. "Well, at least it's black. I look good in black."

Lou glanced over at him, his comments eliciting a reluctant chuckle from her. "Well, thank God for that."

Rolly smiled. "So Lou, being we're going to be fellow cult members, why don't you tell me a little about yourself?"

"Uh, like what?"

Rolly shrugged. "I don't know. Is this your first cult experience?"

Lou smiled in spite of the terror she felt. "Why yes. Yes it is."

"Me too. We must not get out enough. Any idea where we're headed?"

Lou shrugged. "Pascha said he picked it. That's all I know. And that he thought we'd all really like it."

Rolly looked to the front of the van. "Hm, I'm going to go out on a limb and say his tastes and my tastes probably don't coincide all that much."

"Yeah. I think you're probably right on that."

Twenty minutes later, their suspicions were confirmed.

"You have got to be kidding," Lou muttered staring at the building that loomed in the distance.

"We're staying there?" Rolly asked.

"God, I hope not."

But the van was heading in an unerring straight line. A three story Gothic inspired mansion appeared in the distance. A giant tower loomed in the center and two wings grew out of the sides. It looked like something out of a horror movie.

They passed a sign and Lou knew her eyes had gotten even bigger. She grabbed Rolly's arm. "Did you see that?"

"What?" Rolly asked.

"The sign. It said Danvers State Insane Asylum."

Rolly's head swiveled toward her, his eyes bright. "Danvers? Seriously?"

Lou nodded.

"Holy crap, that *is* actually kind of cool."

"Cool?" Lou asked wondering if she had misread Rolly.

"No, I mean it's creepy. But this was the place that inspired H.P. Lovecraft. It actually started out as a cool place, where they were really concerned about patient care. But eventually it became crowded. In fact, it got so crowded that patients sometimes died and weren't discovered for days. And they became the poster children for lobotomies and shock therapy. It closed down back in the early nineties. It hasn't been used since."

Lou felt even more uneasy than she had even a few minutes ago. "And you know this why?"

Rolly regarded her for a minute before speaking. "My mom, she uh, she was institutionalized when I was six. She spent two years inside a hospital like this. They finally figured out the right drug combo and she was released. But she was in and out of hospitals for most of her life. So I did a lot of research on psychology and hospitals and stuff."

"I'm sorry," Lou said.

Rolly shrugged. "We all have our stories, right?"

Lou thought about Charlotte, her mom, and grandmother. Five years and they were all gone. Five years was the time it took to take her from a happy home to the back of a van heading toward a creeped out hospital for some sort of training camp run by psychos.

Lou's voice was soft when she spoke. "Yeah. We do."

They didn't have any more time for conversation though as the van pulled to a stop a few feet from the front door.

"Wow and I thought it was creepy from afar," Rolly muttered.

Mortar was chipped in between the bricks and weeds ravaged the front. The windows that could be seen were either boarded up or broken. Lou glanced out the van window and up, expecting bats to come flying out of the windows. Seconds later, a few did.

All of the occupants in the van were stunned into silence.

Pascha turned around, his smile huge. "Great, right?"

No one said anything but Pascha didn't seem to mind or notice. "Wait until you see the inside. It's even better."

Everyone exited the van. Lou was the second to last to get out. She stepped out and stared up at the building, wrapping her arms around herself.

Rolly stopped next to her, whispering. "Um, I think I might have made a mistake."

Lou looked up at him. "Yeah. Me too."

CHAPTER 43

Amazingly, the inside of the hospital was worse than the outside. At least outside, the sunlight helped it be not quite as despairing. Inside, with most of the windows covered, it was beyond depressing - it was sinister.

Pascha quickly hustled them through the first floor. Lou glanced into what had been a parlor at one time, with dark moldings and a giant fireplace. She could imagine it back in its day, looking strangely elegant.

Pascha, though, didn't take time to give them a tour. He moved them quickly down the halls. Lou caught glimpses of rooms as she passed. It was eerie. Like everyone had just picked up and left one day. There was still some furniture left behind - even a few pieces of clothing and papers scattered about.

And there were lots of guards - some human, some not. Lou swallowed. Getting out of here was not going to be easy. She thought of Jen. Getting in here wasn't going to be easy either.

Pascha led them straight to the east wing on the third floor. And the only reason Lou knew it was the east wing was due to the decrepit sign announcing it.

The windows weren't covered which allowed them to see more. Although after seeing the peeling plaster, rooms with old beds and remnants of hospital equipment, Lou wasn't sure that was a good thing. This must have been where the more difficult patients were kept.

Lou expected an old patient to drift down the hall toward them, sans eyes and a soul. No wonder Lovecraft had been inspired by the place. And that was during its heyday. If he visited today, his horror stories would be even more terrifying.

She glanced around as a wind blew through the hall. A chill stole over her. *Or maybe he does still visit - along with some friends.*

They passed through a set of double doors and to their right was a Plexiglas window. On the other side was a chair with straps.

"Hello, Clarice," Rolly whispered down to her.

Lou rolled her eyes, but still felt goose bumps break out across her skin.

Pascha paused at an open doorway and waved them all in. "Ah, here we are."

As Lou stepped through she realized this room must have been a ward at one point, due to its size. Old beds were lined along the cracked walls. There were already about ten kids there in the back of the room. They were wearing the same tracksuits and seemed to have already claimed their spots.

Pascha waved them forward. "Go ahead. Choose a bed."

The new kids spread out slowly. Lou and Rolly picked two beds near the door.

Rolly smacked his bed and a layer of dust rose in the air. "Wow. They really went all out in accommodations," he muttered.

"Yeah," Lou said. "I was promised something a little more luxurious."

The other teens who'd ridden with them looked equally unimpressed.

One of the girls tossed her blonde hair over her shoulder. "I am *not* staying in this dump."

Everyone went silent.

Pascha tilted his head. "Did someone have a comment to make?"

The girl stepped forward. "I did. I'm not staying here. This place is gross."

Pascha walked over to her.

Lou choked down the warning in her throat. She could tell the girl didn't have any abilities, at least not yet.

Pascha smiled. Before anyone could breathe, he wrapped his arms around her neck and twisted.

The crack resounded through the room.

He let her go. She dropped to the floor - her eyes open, staring accusingly at them all.

Lou gasped and she felt Rolly stiffen beside her.

Pascha just smiled, his eyes cold. "Now, let me make clear the rules. You are here to prove that you are worthy. She-" He nodded toward the body on the floor, "was not. If you'd like to survive, make sure that you are."

CHAPTER 44

Henry drove down the highway looking for some sign of the van. He kept his eyes peeled to the road but every once in a while he couldn't help but glance at Jen. She looked so pale. He knew if anything happened to Lou it would kill her.

His phone beeped and he glanced to where it was attached to the dashboard. Danny.

He hit the speaker. "Danny? Do you have anything?"

Jen sat up straight in the chair next to him, but then seemed to deflate at Danny's first words.

"I'm still looking for the van. But I do have an ID on the guy who Lou met up with."

Jen leaned forward. "Who is he?"

"His name is Pascha Bukin," a female voice said.

"Laney?" Jen asked.

"Yes. You guys should have told me what you were planning."

Henry glanced over at Jen. "We wanted to give you a little break from all this. It's been a tough year."

"Yeah. But you still should have told me. Jake's already on the way to you. If not for Kati and Max, I'd be there too. But enough about that, the guy who recruited Lou has a rather horrific back story."

"How'd you find him?" Jen asked.

"Danny ran his face through facial rec and then I ran his name through the FBI database. And surprise, surprise, our guy has a record."

"What's he done?" Henry asked.

"Lots - a string of juvenile arrests but most of the charges were dropped. Witnesses had an unhappy habit of disappearing. And although he was suspected in a number of adult crimes, no one has ever been able to get the charges to stick."

Jen closed her eyes.

Henry pictured the boy that had taken Lou. "Wait, did you say adult crimes? Doesn't he have to be eighteen to be charged?"

"No. In most states now, you can be charged as an adult when you turn sixteen, especially for the tougher crimes. But that's not what's happening here. Your guy is not a juvenile."

Jen's eyes flew open. "What? He looks like he's in junior high at most."

"Well, you've seen from the stills, he's short. He wasn't supposed to be. But apparently his mother locked him to a radiator for years. His height is due to malnutrition. Even though he only looks like he's around twelve, he's actually twenty."

Henry looked at Jen in shock. "Twenty?"

"His mother," Laney continued, "was not exactly mother of the year. There's actually a pretty well documented history of him from CPS."

"What did she do, besides the radiator?"

"Lots of physical abuse - but also emotional abuse. For example, mommy dearest sent Pascha to the first day of kindergarten in a dress, complete with hair ribbons, as a punishment for breaking one of his toys."

"Oh my God," Jen mumbled.

Laney blew out a breath. "Trust me, that was one of her least horrendous deeds. The others range from sexual abuse to cigarette burns to even more that I'll keep to myself to spare you the nightmares."

"Anyway, his mother was killed when he was twelve. When the police arrived, little Pascha, who only weighed forty pounds, was sitting at the kitchen table eating a bowl of cereal. His mom was sitting in a chair in the living room with over a dozen stab wounds."

"He's the one killing the women," Jen said slowly.

"Yeah," Laney agreed. "And not to get all profiler on you, but he's killing his mother over and over again."

Henry felt the horror crawl over him. "Laney, what does that kind of background do to a person?"

Laney's voice was heavy with concern. "It depends. No one could be unaffected by that kind of early trauma. But it depends on what direction their personality was pointed at birth. For some, they'll become introverted, no sense of self, no self-esteem. They'll be drawn to relationships that victimize them again and again."

"But that's not this guy," Jen said.

Laney's voice was emphatic. "No. That's not Pascha. He's the type that lashes out. You need to get the kids away from him. And while I generally would say that you should try and catch him and send him to Clark, I don't believe that's the best scenario here."

Laney paused and when she spoke, her voice was deadly serious. "If you get the chance, you need to make sure he doesn't have a chance to harm anyone else. Do you know what I mean?"

Henry glanced over at Jen whose face had gone white. For Laney to make that kind of statement was unusual to say the least. "Yeah, Laney. We know," Henry said.

CHAPTER 45

Lou walked toward the body carrying a sheet. Pascha had picked her and Rolly for body disposal duty.

Pascha nodded down the hall. "There's a grassy area out back - one floor down. Just dump her there. The rats will enjoy her."

Lou struggled to keep her revulsion off her face. Rolly wasn't as good at hiding his.

They placed the sheet next to the body and then rolled the girl into it. *I'm sorry,* Lou thought as she wrapped the material around her.

Following Pascha's direction, they carried the body through the hall and down a flight of stairs. Lou tried to tell herself it was a rug but it wasn't possible to keep the reality out. Lou felt her stomach heave more than once as she made her way down the stairs. Kicking open a rusty door, Rolly stepped out into an old courtyard and Lou followed.

Lou paused. "Um, where do you think we should put her?"

Rolly nodded toward the back corner. "How about over there?"

Lou nodded and headed over. They put the body down and then cleared a space, placing the girl in it.

Lou grabbed a couple of sheets of wood off the windows nearby, covering the body. Rolly did the same.

They stepped back. It wouldn't keep many animals out, but it was the best they could do for now.

Rolly stood with his hands on his waist. He looked back at the building and then at Lou. "What the hell was that back there?"

Lou glanced over at him. Rolly looked really shaken - a lot more shaken then some of the other people had looked.

Lou glanced around to make sure no one could overhear them. She took a step toward Rolly and lowered her voice. "Look, whatever you do, don't let them see how much this got to you. I don't think Pascha's someone you want to show weakness to."

Rolly fixed her with a gaze. "Why do I get the feeling you know more about what's happening here than you're letting on?"

Lou looked away.

"Not everybody here has abilities, do they?" Rolly asked.

"No, they don't."

"And you can tell who does?"

Lou nodded.

"So do some have more abilities than others?"

Lou looked back at him. "I don't think so. From what I understand, there are two types of us. I can tell who has abilities. You can only read your type."

"The electric shock?"

Lou nodded. "Look, Rolly, you seem like a nice guy, so be careful okay? If you're scared, mad, whatever - don't let them see that."

Rolly was silent for a moment watching Lou. Finally, he nodded. "Okay."

Lou gestured to the door. "We should get back."

The two of them jogged back across the courtyard and up the stairs. They stepped out onto the landing just as Pascha stepped out of the dorm room.

"Excellent. Just in time," Pascha said.

"Uh, what are we doing?" Lou asked.

Pascha smiled. "Beginning your training."

CHAPTER 46

Training, Lou thought with disgust. *More like the Pascha show.*

Pascha had led them into the gymnasium downstairs. Spotlights had been hooked up so that they could see. It was the only place in the hospital where they had done so. Lou had the uncomfortable feeling that Pascha expected them to spend most of their time here.

Pascha walked around the front of the circle that had been painted on the old floor. "We are not like other humans. We do not need to snivel by - looking for crumbs. We were given our abilities for a purpose - to take what we want. Let me show you."

He moved to the middle of the ring as two men were led in. Each was above six feet tall and heavily muscled. From the homemade tattoos that adorned their arms, Lou was pretty sure they were ex-cons.

Pascha grinned at the men, waving them forward.

Lou felt nauseous again. She could tell neither of the men had abilities. She bit her lip and glanced around. There were four other guards in the room, each with guns. Even if she managed to help the two men, the guards would kill her. And them as well.

Rolly leaned down to her. "Can either of them fight him?"

Lou shook her head but kept her eyes focused on Pascha. "No."

One of the men charged. Pascha stood still and then stepped aside unleashing a vicious sidekick to the man's ribs. He screamed and grabbed his side.

The other attacked him from behind, wrapping his arms around Pascha and lifting him off his feet. Latching onto the man's neck, Pascha curled up his legs and then flung them to the floor, dropping all of his weight.

The man pitched forward. His skull smacked the ground with a sharp crack.

Pascha flung him away.

The man didn't move.

Pascha walked over to his friend, who held up his hands. "No, please."

Next to her, Rolly started to stand.

Lou yanked him down. "Don't. You can't help him."

"We have to try."

Lou shook her head, but didn't look at Rolly. Pascha kicked the man in the face then walked around him. Pascha raised his foot above the man's head.

Lou closed her eyes so she didn't see the stomp. But she heard it. It echoed through the silent room.

And Lou knew she would hear it every night for the rest of her life.

CHAPTER 47

AFTER PASCHA'S LITTLE DEMONSTRATION, it was dinnertime. An hour earlier, Lou would have devoured the pizza in front of her. But now she had no appetite. She forced herself to take a bite, though, because Pascha was watching all of them for their reaction. Lou was comforted to see a few other people looked a little green as well.

Lou and Rolly sat away from the rest of the group but that wasn't a problem. They weren't exactly a cohesive unit. Most people seemed to be keeping to themselves.

Twenty minutes later, Lou dropped her slice back on her plate. She'd eaten half of it and that was about as much as she could choke down. She glanced over at Rolly's plate. His full slice sat untouched. Rolly stared off into space.

"You really should eat something," Lou said softly.

Rolly looked back at her. "He killed those men. And we didn't stop him."

Lou looked around but no one was close enough to hear and Pascha had disappeared somewhere. "I know but we are way outnumbered."

"Outnumbered? How do you know that?"

Lou glanced around. "You got a slight electric sensation when you saw some of the others, right?"

Rolly nodded.

"Well, I get a much bigger one. There are a lot more guards here than you realize. If we said or did anything, we'd be dead right along side those two men."

Rolly's jaw dropped and he stared at her for a moment. Then he shook his head. "Pascha's evil. They're all evil."

Lou nodded. Rolly was right - it was evil. And they were going to have to figure a way out of here soon. Because there was no way she could sit through another one of Pascha's 'demonstrations.'

Lou remembered what Maddox had told her about the camps he'd been in. They tried to find out early on who had the stomach for this kind of work, although how they did that varied by camp. Lou did not want to find out what Pascha's method was going to be.

She glanced up at Rolly. "Why are you here? Most people here are kind of jerks. But you're not."

"I could say the same for you," Rolly said, his eyes downcast.

"I suppose you could." Lou paused. Should she tell him why she was really here? Could she trust him?

Rolly looked out the window. "You know, I have an older sister."

"You do? You only mentioned the younger one."

Rolly shook his head. "Alicia - she's the older one. Her and I got split up in foster care. She called me about a year ago. Said someone had come to her. Said he had a place for her to go where she'd fit in."

"What happened?"

"I never heard from her again. When I was approached I knew it was the same people. I'm not here for me. I need to know what happened to her."

Lou felt a lump in her throat. "I'm sorry Rolly."

He shrugged. "I'm guessing my stories no sadder than yours."

Lou gave him a brief smile. "No, I guess it's not." She hesitated for only a few seconds. She took a deep breath. "My sister's name was Charlotte." And the whole story poured out of her.

When Lou was done, Rolly looked around, keeping his voice low. "So these people, this Jen, they've gotten people out of camps like this before?"

"Yeah. I had a tracker on me but I lost it when we got changed at that rest area." She pictured Jen. "But they're looking for me, for all of us."

"If they've gotten people out of camps, they might know what happened to Alicia."

"They might."

Rolly nodded and Lou could sense his resolve. "Okay. So now we just need to figure out a way to contact them. Let them know we're here. Any ideas?"

Lou shook her head. "Well, ideally we could just call them and tell them where we are. Then they arrive with guns blazing."

Rolly paused. He glanced at Lou, an eyebrow raised. "They took all our cells. But I've seen a few of the guards with cell phones. So we just need to get one of theirs."

"Okay - but how? I don't think they're just going to hand one over."

Rolly grinned. "I guess that just depends on how we ask."

CHAPTER 48

Lou lay in her cot, trying not to imagine all the bugs that were undeniably living there. She listened to the room, but it had gone silent about a half hour ago. All she could hear was even breathing.

The cot next to hers creaked and Rolly snuck over to her bed. "Ready?" he whispered.

Lou nodded and quickly got out of her bed. Quietly, they crept out of the room. There were some electric lanterns placed around the halls, making it easier to see. They knew there was a guard at the end of the hall - a human guard.

Lou snuck down the hall with Rolly behind her. She tried not to think about the people that had lived here years ago or the fact that she was acting out the beginning of about a dozen slasher movies she'd seen.

On the other side of the door, the guard leaned against the wall, his back to them. Lou glanced through the door. He was playing a game on his phone - Candy Crush.

Rolly looked at her and Lou nodded. Taking a breath, Rolly straightened and pushed through the doors, heading down the hall. "Hey man."

"Where do you think you're going?" the guard asked shoving his phone in his pocket.

"Just stretching my legs." Rolly stretched his arms above his head once he was on the other side of the man.

The guard nudged his head back toward the door. "Yeah, well no stretching. Get back inside."

Lou snuck out the door while the man's back was to her. Moving fast, she reached up and wrapped her arm around his neck. She locked it in place with her other arm like Jordan had taught her.

"What the-?" The man tried to slam her against the wall, but Rolly pinned him in place. Thirty seconds later, the man was unconscious. Quickly, they searched him and found the phone in his pocket.

Lou pulled it out quickly dialing Jen's number as they made their way to the stairwell. They were heading to the back of the hospital. Lou had sensed fewer guards back there - which might mean there were more human guards. But she still preferred their odds with the human guards.

They needed to get out of the hospital now. As soon as the guard woke up, he was going to tell everyone what they had done. The only way to avoid that was to kill him and neither she nor Rolly was prepared for that.

The call connected.

"Who is this?" Jen's voice was riddled with static.

Lou nearly cried with relief. "Jen. It's me. It's Lou."

"Lou - are - ?" The phone died.

Lou stared at it in disbelief.

"What happened?"

"I lost the signal."

Rolly closed his eyes. "Seriously?"

Lou nodded. "We're really not great at this spy stuff are we?"

"Well, it got through. That's what matters. And if you're right about a genius on the other end, he should be able to trace it, right?"

Lou nodded, thinking of Danny. He'd be able to trace it. And on TV, they always made tracing a call look simple. "You're right. Plus, when we get outside, we'll probably be able to pick up a signal again. Now we just need to get out of here without getting caught."

"Easy," Rolly said, quietly pulling open the door to the first floor.

The beam of a flashlight caught them as soon as they stepped through. "Just where do you two think you're going?"

Hallway lanterns made it bright enough to see Pascha's angry face.

"Or maybe not," Rolly muttered.

CHAPTER 49

DANNY TRACED the call to the nearest cell phone tower - the area covered was only a few square miles. He was working to get an exact location but Jen wasn't waiting. She and Henry had the whole group converge on the city of Danvers.

Jen urged the car forward. "Come on." *Ten minutes away, Lou had only been ten minutes away this whole time.*

Henry's phone beeped and Jen snatched it up. "What have you got?"

Laney's voice rang out through the car. "I can't be sure but I think I may have found your spot. Danny's -" she paused "borrowing a satellite feed to get some heat signatures."

"What's the place?" Henry asked.

"Danvers State Insane Asylum," Laney said.

"An Asylum?" Jen asked.

"It's been out of commission for years. In fact, it's slated to be turned into apartments in a couple of months. But it's within range of the cell phone tower. And I think it would appeal to Pascha."

"Twisted little freak," Jen muttered.

"Exactly," Laney said. "Hold on."

Jen could hear excited murmuring in the background but she couldn't make out any of the conversation.

Laney got back on the phone. "Danny found the heat signatures. There are at least forty of them. About ten are ringed around the perimeter of the building."

Jen closed her eyes. "Okay. What else?"

"There are two white vans parked round the back of the building. It's them, Jen."

"Henry?" Jen asked.

He nodded, pressing the accelerator down.

"Go get them," Laney said before disconnecting.

Jen quickly dialed the rest of the group and gave them the coordinates.

Henry glanced at her from the side of his eyes. "We'll get her out."

Jen nodded, but wasn't able to speak right then.

They'd get to Lou in time. They had to.

CHAPTER 50

Pascha threw Lou into the middle of the ring in the gymnasium. Two other men threw Rolly.

Lou got up slowly. She stared at the faces of the people around them. After catching her and Rolly, Pascha had raised the alarm. Guards had surrounded them within seconds.

They'd been marched to the gymnasium. The rest of the teens had also been marched here. Apparently, Pascha didn't want them to miss the show.

Pascha strode around the edge of the circle. "These two have broken the rules. More than that, they assaulted one of my men."

He glared at the group. Most wouldn't meet his eyes. Lou saw a tremor run through more than one of them.

Pascha pointed at Rolly who was just getting to his feet. "Who did you call?"

Rolly dusted off his pants. "Pizza guy. I've been having such a craving for a stuffed crust."

Pascha nodded to one of the armed men who walked over and slammed the butt of his assault rifle into Rolly's stomach.

With a grunt, Rolly crashed to his knees - the air knocked out of him. The man moved to hit him again. Lou ran over and shoved him away. She stood in front of Rolly, glaring at Pascha and the guard.

Genuine enjoyment splashed across Pascha's face. He pointed at Lou. "You see that? That's what we're looking for - people with courage - people who are willing to lay it on the line. Of course, these two are complete traitors and therefore absolutely useless to us, but you get the idea."

Rolly got to his feet and stood next to Lou, his hand briefly touching hers. Lou gave him a subtle nod, but didn't take her eyes off Pascha.

Pascha looked back at Lou and Rolly, his eyes wide, his smile big. He clapped his hands together. "I've just had a wonderful idea! A way they can help us."

Lou's stomach tightened.

"How about we use them as a demonstration? I usually save this for later in in the training, but I think the lesson may need to be learned earlier. You see - we like to ease you into the process. But eventually, you need to prove your worth. You need to defeat one of your fellow trainees."

Rolly sucked in a breath. Lou felt sick. They wanted her to fight Rolly. She wouldn't do it. She couldn't.

Pascha paused studying Lou and Rolly. "You two are thinking you won't fight each other, right?"

Neither Lou nor Rolly said anything.

Pascha slapped his knee. "I knew it. But don't worry. You don't have to. Keith, Hans."

Two giant guards stepped forward, their expressions eager.

Pascha smiled. "You get to fight them."

CHAPTER 51

THE SCENERY BLEW by Jen in a blur. She glanced over at the odometer. It was hitting one hundred and ten miles per hour.

And she still wished Henry would go faster.

Ahead, the insane asylum was silhouetted against the dark night sky. *This place is huge,* Jen thought, her confidence dimming.

As they got closer, Jen could sense the nephilim inside. Which meant they could sense her. Five minutes earlier, Jake had led a human task force in to take out the perimeter guards and that had gone smoothly. They didn't think any of the guards had had the chance to raise the alarm.

But now the Fallen would know they were coming. Their only chance was that maybe they were distracted by something else and wouldn't pick up on the signals until too late. But it was two in the morning, what could possibly distract them at this time?

Henry slammed to a stop in front of the main doors. Jordan was already there - waiting.

Jen handed Henry a shotgun. He took it, catching her hand. She looked up into his eyes. "We've got this," he said.

Jen banished all doubt from her mind. "Damn right we do."

CHAPTER 52

Lou stood with her back against Rolly's in the center of the ring. Hans and Keith circled around them.

"Lou?" Rolly asked.

"They're both nephilim," Lou whispered, not taking her eyes off of Hans who was circling toward her.

"Well at least Pascha didn't let them use guns," Rolly said. "That's a plus."

Lou watched Hans. "Yeah but he did let them use their knives." Each man had a knife strapped to his waist but neither had reached for it. Apparently they wanted to use their fists first.

As Pascha had explained, guns would have ended the fight too quickly. But with knives, the fun could go on and on.

"True," Rolly said. "But we have full blown terror on our side. That has to count for something."

The laugh was strangled in her throat. Hans charged. Behind her, she could here Keith doing the same. "Jump," Lou yelled.

As if they practiced it, Lou and Rolly leapt in the air, landing behind each of their assailants. But they had no time to appreciate the beauty of their move. Hans swiveled like he'd expected the action and slammed into Lou, sending her sprawling.

Keith grabbed Rolly and slammed him to the ground. With a vicious kick in the ribs, he sent Rolly rolling across the floor.

Rolly crashed into Lou. Stumbling, she grabbed him and helped him stand.

Rolly grunted. "Okay, so got any more ideas?"

Lou narrowed her eyes. "Yeah. Let's stop playing defense." She ran for Hans, faking a punch to the face before dropping and sliding through his legs. She slammed her fist right into his groin.

Hans groaned but didn't fall. "You're going to pay for that."

Lou smiled back at him. "Try your best, buddy."

Hans smiled. Lou heard the foot fall the second before Keith grabbed her shoulder. But Rolly tackled Keith away from her, slamming him to the ground and punching him repeatedly. "It's. Not. Nice. To. Hit. A. Girl."

Lou's attention on Rolly gave Hans the opening he needed. A straight punch sent Lou flying and she was sure her jaw was broken. She grunted, tasting blood in her mouth.

Pascha knelt down near her. "Tsk, tsk, tsk - not looking good there, Lou."

Lou spit a wad of blood in his face.

In a split second, Pascha's face went from smirk to incensed. He grabbed Lou by the hair and yanked her up.

Pain screeched through her scalp. He punched her in the face twice. Lou's head snapped back and consciousness winked out for a moment. She blinked furiously trying to stabilize her vision.

Pascha's eyes narrowed and his cheeks flamed with color. He spit out his words. "You bitch."

The sound of gunfire made him pause.

Lou smiled back at him as the pain in her face began to recede. "I believe they're here for me."

Pascha pulled his fist back. The punch sent Lou sailing through the air. She landed in a heap, and saw Rolly land on the ground across the ring.

Pascha stomped toward her. He gestured to one of the guards who handed over his gun. Pascha aimed it at Lou. "Say goodbye."

CHAPTER 53

Jen sprinted through the building. Jake, Yoni and their team were clearing out any remaining guards. That was their priority. Maddox, Henry, Jordan, and Jen were searching for the kids. Danny said most of the heat signatures were grouped at the back of the building.

As they got closer, Jen could sense the nephilim. She poured on the speed but Maddox outpaced her. Not waiting for Henry and Jen to catch up he burst through the door into the gym.

Jen was right behind him - the butt of her P90 tucked into her shoulder.

Lou was on the ground. Pascha stood over her with his gun pointed at her heart.

Jen took it all in in a second - the same amount of time it took her to pull the trigger.

Pascha stumbled back again and again as bullets slammed into him. The rest of the kids in the gym stumbled away, running for the doors.

Henry, Jordan, and Maddox focused on the other guards in the room.

Jen only had eyes for Lou. She ran to her and fell to her knees at Lou's side. "Lou? Lou?"

Lou turned her head.

Jen blanched at the bruises even though she knew they'd heal. The healing never mitigated the pain in receiving them.

Jen felt the tears burn the back of her throat. "Oh God Lou, I'm sorry."

Lou struggled to her knees. "You came."

Jen pulled Lou into her arms. "Of course I came."

Lou stiffened for a moment and then she wrapped her arms around Jen. "You came," she said again. Then her shoulders began to shake.

Jen couldn't hug Lou enough. "I'm sorry. I'm sorry. I'm so sorry."

Lou just clung to Jen tighter.

The boy who'd been on the other side of the floor made his way over. He sat gingerly on the floor next to them. "Any of those hugs for me?"

Lou pulled away and with tears streaming down her face, pulled him into a hug. Finally breaking apart, Lou wiped at her cheeks.

"Guess we showed them," he said, a grimace as he held his side.

Lou laughed. "Guess we did." She turned to Jen. "This is Rolly. He's the reason you found us."

The grimace on Rolly's face faded. "True. It was all me."

Lou whacked him on the arm.

Rolly sighed. "Fine. Lou helped a little."

Jen extended her hand. "It is very nice to meet you Rolly."

Rolly's face turned serious as he took Jen's hand. "Thank you for saving us."

Jen nodded, a catch at the back of her throat. "You are very welcome."

CHAPTER 54

Henry stood in the parking lot of the Marriot in Danvers. He'd rented out every room that wasn't occupied. They had gathered up twenty kids who ranged in age from twelve to nineteen.

A few had had to be hospitalized. Nothing serious luckily - one kid had run into the middle of a firefight, but he'd only been grazed. There were a few broken bones, one case of malnutrition, and one asthma attack. And obviously, none of those kids had any powers yet. And maybe never would.

They'd taken out most of Pascha's force - capturing over a dozen of them. The SIA agents had taken away the eight Fallen and nephilim they'd caught. The humans had all been hospitalized and then they'd head to jail to await trial.

Tomorrow, they'd figure out what to do with all of the kids. But right now, they all needed to sleep and eat, not necessarily in that order. All in all, it had gone better than expected.

The only fly in the ointment was that Pascha had escaped. Due to his height, some members of the force had thought he was one of the teenagers. He managed to sneak through their lines and off the grounds of the asylum.

Henry had forwarded his picture and information to every law enforcement agency with the instructions not to approach him but to contact SIA. Henry had the feeling, however, that the next time they saw Pascha it would be because Pascha chose to be seen.

Yoni walked up to Henry. "Tsk, tsk, tsk."

Henry glanced down at him, his eyebrows raised. "What are you tsking at?"

"You." Yoni nodded toward Jen who stood surrounded by the teenagers. Although she was taking notes from all of them, she kept scanning the group every few seconds to check on Lou. "And her."

"What do you mean?" Henry asked.

Yoni shook his head. "You are in very real danger of falling into the friend zone."

"What? I'm not-"

Yoni put up his hand. "Look, you are smarter than me. I do not deny that. You are more successful than me. I give you that too. But with women, your track record is horrible."

"Yoni, what are you-"

"Hey - I'm not saying this to make you feel bad. I'm just saying, you know, have you met my wife?"

Henry pictured Sasha Benjamin, who now helped run the Chandler School. Almost six feet tall with long blonde hair, Sasha had been an Olympic volleyball player for the Ukraine two Olympics ago. She was also incredibly smart and empathetic.

Henry nodded stiffly.

"Right, so I'd say in that area, I'm ahead of you. So take some advice from a man who has found the woman that makes his life worth living - don't wait. Tell her." Yoni walked away and Henry watched him go.

The little Israeli might appear to some to be all brash, but he noticed more than people gave him credit for.

Henry turned back and watched Jen as she handed out room keys. As each teenager grabbed a key, they disappeared into the hotel.

"No mini bar!" Jen yelled but there was a smile on her face. She gave the last key to Rolly.

Lou looked up at her. "What about me?"

"You're bunking with me," Jen said. "If that's okay."

Lou nodded with a smile. "Okay with me."

Rolly nudged Lou. "Come on. Let's go get something to eat. I'm starving."

Linking arms with Rolly, Lou looked at Jen. "Want to join us?"

Jen glanced over at Henry and then back at the kids. "I'll be in in a little bit."

"Okay," Lou said before heading inside with Rolly.

Henry took a breath and walked over to Jen. She turned around and smiled at him. "Well, they should have all started running up their room service bills by now."

Henry smiled with a shrug. "I think that's the least they deserve after what they've been through."

"True." She paused. "You want to go for a walk?"

Henry nodded. "That'd be great."

They walked down the block and stumbled across a park. A man-made lake had been placed in the center with trees scattered along its edge. Jen and Henry stepped onto a small deck overlooking it. Ducks swam by and a few flew by overhead.

Henry looked down at Jen as she leaned against the railing. In profile, she was stunning. He could not recall ever seeing anyone more beautiful.

He turned back to the water. Yoni's words tumbled through his mind. *You're heading into the friend zone.* "Are you okay?"

Jen nodded turning to him. "Yeah. Lou's safe and so are the rest of them. So yeah, I'm good."

Jen looked back at the water a smile on her face. Henry stared at her for a moment feeling completely tongue-tied.

"Hey Henry?" Jen asked softly.

He turned to find her looking up at him. "Yeah?"

"Are you *ever* going to kiss me?"

Henry felt his mouth drop open. "I didn't think-"

Jen wound her arms around Henry's neck. "Stop thinking."

Henry lowered his head to hers. "Yes ma'am."

CHAPTER 55

DELANEY MCPHEARSON DISCONNECTED the call and looked over at her uncle, Father Patrick Delaney. "They're all okay. They got there in time."

Patrick closed his eyes. "Thank goodness." He bowed his head and Laney knew he was praying.

The morning sun made Patrick's red hair appear even redder. Laney had always thought she got her own red hair from Patrick's side of the family. But like a lot of things she learned in the last two years, that hadn't been entirely correct.

She closed her eyes and sent her own informal message out to the universe. *Thank you.*

She stood up and stretched. They were sitting on the back porch of Laney's cottage on the Chandler Estate. Kati was inside putting Max to sleep.

Laney breathed deep with a smile. This was truly a 'life is good' moment.

Patrick came to stand next to her, wrapping his hand in hers. "When will all the kids be arriving?"

"In the next few days. We'll have to see legally where each kid stands. Some of the kids are in the hospital but nothing serious.

Jake thinks at least a dozen of the kids will be heading back here with us. We'll have to get some beds set up."

"Shouldn't be a problem. There's plenty of space."

Laney nodded, a feeling of contentment in her chest. This was the first time she hadn't been involved in a Fallen incident. It had been hard to stay away. But Kati, Max, the kids at the school - they all needed her too.

And in the end, everything had turned out fine. Maybe she could delegate a little bit more. Let some other people handle things. Let her and Jake have a life.

Lines from the book they had recovered from Amar's estate flashed across her mind:

The time of judgment is at hand.

The choice of sacrifice or death will be made.

Laney shoved the thoughts aside. She didn't know what the words referred to. And right now, she didn't want to. She just wanted to relish this one moment when the world was calm.

Laney leaned into her uncle's shoulder with a sigh.

He patted her hand. "What's the sigh for?"

"All of it. I wasn't shot at. All of our people are all right. And the kids are safe. And there are no looming crises. For once, everything is peaceful."

EPILOGUE

ATLANTA, GEORGIA

THE LITTLE BLONDE girl played in her front yard. The man in the car two houses down looked at the folder in front of him. Sophia Watson, age ten. He handed the photo to the man in the passenger seat.

"That her?" The passenger asked.

The driver nodded. "So what do you think?" The two could pass for brothers with their dark brown hair, light brown eyes, and muscular build.

The passenger glanced up and down the block. "Blocks pretty quiet. We can grab her from here. But we should probably wait until night."

The driver pointed to the house across the street. "There's a little old lady there who seems to be always parked at her window - watching. Night would be better."

The passenger looked at the little girl, who was playing hopscotch on the front walk. Sun glinted off her almost white hair and her smile was huge. He shook his head. "It's hard to believe she's one of them."

The driver nodded. His lip curled in distaste. "But she is. A wolf in sheep's clothing."

The passenger nodded. "'The way of the wicked is an abomination to the Lord'."

The driver made the sign of the cross. "Let God's will be done."

―――

Delaney McPhearson's journey continues in The Belial Children. Now available on Amazon

FACT OR FICTION

I know, I know - I use very little history and/or archaeology in this story. In my defense, I never intended for Lou's story to be a stand-alone novel. Originally, Lou was part of the next book, *The Belial Children*. But as *The Belial Children* developed, I realized there were too many story lines and one needed to be dropped. Lou made the most sense. But I still really liked her.

As a result, *Recruit* was born. And while there is little archaeology, there is some truth that I drew from to create the tale. Enjoy!

The Death of Rasputin. I actually wrote a scene for *The Belial Library* that depicted the death of Rasputin. Maybe it will appear in some future book. Rasputin's death was fascinating without any embellishment. As described in *Recruit*, Rasputin was indeed shot, stabbed, poisoned and finally drowned.

According to historians, after he ingested poison laced pastries, Rasputin appeared even more chipper. After finally, being stabbed and shot, he was tied into a rug and tossed in the Neva River. When his body was found a few days later, one of his arms had worked its way free of the ropes - leading some to speculate, that Rasputin had still been alive when tossed in.

Martin Luther King High School. The high school I describe Lou attending in Detroit is actually taken from descriptions of some of the worst high schools in the United States. If you're looking for a great book on the horrible state of public schools at one end of the economic spectrum, check out *Savage Inequalities* by Jonathon Kozol. In fact, some of the worst schools in *Savage Inequalities* are named Martin Luther King High School.

Danvers State Insane Asylum. The Danvers State Asylum is an actual insane asylum. It is closed down now. In fact, parts of it have been renovated into apartments. But the history and description of the asylum are accurate: It is a Gothic styled mansion. You expect thunder to clap and lightning to slash across the sky, as well as for the sky to be perpetually grey above it.

The history of lobotomies and shock therapy are also sadly true. In fact, lobotomies were supposed to have been almost perfected there. In addition, there were numerous cases of patients dying and the bodies not being found for days.

The hospital was also one of the inspirations for H.P. Lovecraft. For those unfamiliar with Lovecraft, he is one of the first popular writers of horror.

Pascha. Pascha is obviously a fictional character. But his background is taken from true-life events. Children who have been consistently malnourished do not reach their expected heights. They can be as much as a foot or more shorter than their peers.

Did anyone recognize the description of Pascha's first day of school? A well-known serial killer in fact experienced that. Any guesses? - - - - It was Charles Manson. On his first day of kindergarten, his uncle placed him in a dress because he believed his five-year old nephew wasn't manly enough. In fact, the abuse steeped on Charles Manson during his childhood is horrific.

In fact, it leads to the second factor I used in creating Pascha: while serial killers are very diverse, one thing they all seem to have in common is some form of child abuse.

So Pascha was an amalgamation of all those characteristics. Anyone interested in the backgrounds of serial killers can check out *Whoever Fights Monsters* by Robert Ressler.

THE BELIAL CHILDREN

BOOK 5

AMAZON BEST-SELLING AUTHOR
R.D. BRADY

Keep reading for a peek at *The Belial Children*

THE BELIAL CHILDREN

BALTIMORE, MARYLAND

Delaney McPhearson knew she should focus. It was important. It was life-changing.

She sighed and pushed away from the desk. Who was she kidding? It was paperwork.

She ran her hands through her auburn hair, wishing she'd brought a ponytail holder with her. Her green eyes stared at the desk, imagining what relief one good swipe could bring. But then she imagined herself picking all the papers back up and reorganizing them, and she wanted to scream.

She'd been struggling for the last two hours to reduce the pile on her desk and somehow it only seemed to be getting bigger.

Her eyes roamed over the rich wood paneling that covered the walls, the heavy drapes that contrasted with the more contemporary office furnishings added by the Chandler Group. She was sitting in the administrative offices of the Chandler Home for Children, which had taken over what used to be the Breckenrich School, a well-to-do boarding school that apparently hadn't had enough students to stay afloat.

Laney sighed. *From dodging bullets one minute to filling out forms for Child and Family Services the next. The good times never end.*

The phone rang and Laney grabbed it, looking for a reprieve. "Chandler Home."

"Hi, Ms. McPhearson. This is Leslie from The Bed Place? I'm calling about the order mishap?"

"Hi, Leslie. When will the other beds be delivered?" The last truck had been two beds short.

"Um, well, you see, we have a problem? The beds, they're still at the warehouse?"

Laney rolled her eyes toward the ceiling and prayed for patience. Pulling on her inner calm, she said. "Okay, Leslie, I need those beds here by tomorrow morning."

"I understand. But you see—"

"No, Leslie, you don't understand. I have a dozen kids arriving tomorrow; kids who have literally been through hell. And I mean *hell*. And the least they can expect is to have a bed to sleep in. So do whatever you have to do, but get the beds here tomorrow, understood?"

"Um, yes, Ms. McPhearson. I'll have them there."

"Thank you."

Laney disconnected the call and blew out a breath, feeling a little bad about how she'd bowled over the poor woman. But honestly? She had way too much on her plate right now to be dealing with delivery problems.

Laney stared at the piles of work on her desk. Was it her imagination, or had it actually increased in size while she was on the phone? She ran her hands over her face. *Come on. You need to get this done before the kids arrive tomorrow. They need this.*

And that was true. The Chandler Home for Children had been a haven for Fallen and nephilim teens ever since the Chandler Group took down Amar Patel and learned of a training camp he had set up in Indiana. They'd raided it and liberated the twenty teens that had been held there.

But then the problem had been: what to do with the kids? A

few were over eighteen and had decided to strike out on their own—not that Laney could blame them after what they'd been through—but the others were still minors who either didn't have family or didn't have family they wanted to go back to. And no one could see how dropping the kids in foster care would benefit anyone.

So Henry Chandler, Laney's brother, had purchased this old boarding school about a twenty-minute drive from the Chandler Estate, and dubbed it the Chandler Home for Children. The kids, however, called the home "Broken Halo." Personally, Laney preferred the kids' name.

That first camp in Indiana had led them to another one in Texas, and all told the facility now housed twenty-eight kids ranging in age from twelve to nineteen, more than half of whom had abilities.

Even more kids were expected to arrive soon: a third training camp had been identified just outside Boston, and Laney's love, Jake Rogan, along with Henry and Jennifer Witt, one of Laney's best friends, were off liberating it. That left Laney basically in charge of the school.

She glanced out the window. It was a gorgeous day: bright blue skies, a few white clouds, and a light wind. *Oh, I so want to be anywhere else but here.*

Cleo, the giant black Javan leopard that Laney had rescued from Amar's home, was stretched out in a spot of sunlight behind Laney. When on all fours, Cleo was on eye level with Laney—a result of some growth hormone experiments done on the cat while still in the womb.

In spite of her massive size and intimidating presence, though, Cleo had become part of the school, almost a mascot of sorts. And while the kids had been a little startled by the cat's presence at first, they'd quickly gotten used to her. She was just another facet of Broken Halo.

Laney watched with envy as Cleo let out a yawn and repositioned herself with a lazy stretch. "Oh sure, rub it in," she muttered.

A brunette with a cute pixie cut appeared in the doorway. "Having fun?" Kati Simmons asked.

Laney glanced up with a grimace. "Compared to a root canal? Yes."

Kati walked in and sat in the seat in front of the desk. "Oh, who are you kidding? You love it."

"Don't get me wrong, I love helping the kids out." Laney gestured to all the paperwork. "It's *this* stuff I could do without."

"But someone needs to do it."

"I know, I know." She glanced up at Kati with a grin. "I just heard from the gang. They're ahead of schedule and should return with the kids early tomorrow morning. And Maddox will be back tonight."

Maddox Datson had been an integral part of the last raid, but ever since Amar, he had been staying with Kati and her son Max, as an extra protective bodyguard. When he'd gone off on this latest raid to Boston, Kati and Max had come down from New York to stay with Laney instead—and Laney loved it. She had missed the both of them incredibly over the last year. And these last few weeks reminded her why.

"I just finished setting up the beds for the new kids," Kati said. "Clean linens, towels, a little basket of toiletries for each of them. It should get them started at least."

"You are a godsend." Laney rifled through the pile on the desk. "Jen sent me sizes. I have it here somewhere. I was going to see if Sasha could go to the store and pick them up some clothes and pajamas." Laney looked up just as Kati looked down.

And Laney felt the guilt crash over her again. Ever since the attacks two months ago, Kati had been incredibly nervous about going out in public—hence the need for Maddox's protection.

And Kati's concerns for Max's safety were even greater than her concerns for herself. Laney had really hoped that Kati would begin to feel safe, but so far they'd only made baby steps in that direction.

"You know, we really could use someone like you around here permanently," Laney said.

It was true: Kati had a knack for seeing what needed to be done in the school and taking care of it. And although Laney was more than capable of handling fallen angels, ancient treasures, and hand-to-hand combat, when she was faced with a leaky faucet, she was clueless.

Kati gave Laney a small smile. "I know. I'm thinking about it. And I'm leaning toward moving. It would make things easier. And Maddox can't stay with us forever."

"I don't know. He seems to be enjoying himself."

A small blush colored Kati's cheeks. "Yeah. Somehow he fits right in."

A little boy, five years old and the mini-me of Kati, ran in and threw his arms around Kati's legs. "Hi, Mom!"

Kati's smile was huge. "What have you been up to?"

"Yoni was showing me how to subdue someone with a Chapstick."

Laney stared at Yoni Benjamin, who had appeared in the doorway. Yoni had been part of the Boston raid as well, but he'd come back as soon as the kids were safe. He hated being away from Sasha and their eight-month-old, Dov.

Yoni looked at his feet. "Actually, I was showing Danny. But Max wanted to try, too, and it's important to encourage kids to learn."

Laney shook her head and looked over at Kati, who was looking slightly green. *Great.*

A tall statuesque blonde walked in, tsking at Yoni. "Yoni, I told you not to teach him that. He's too young."

Yoni nodded. "Sorry, sweetie."

Sasha Benjamin leaned down and kissed his bald head. "I love you anyway."

Laney marveled once again at the difference between the two. Sasha had been an Olympic volleyball player a few years back for the Ukraine. She was almost six feet tall and stunningly gorgeous.

Yoni, by contrast, was barely five foot two, with large eyes that dominated his face and biceps the size of willowy Sasha's waist.

On paper, they made no sense. Yet when you saw the two of them together, they just seemed right.

Sasha turned her blue-green eyes to Laney. "Laney, do you have the list?"

Laney rummaged through the papers on her desk and found it under the receipt for the plumber and an order for pizza. *Who ordered pizza?* She shook her head as she handed it over. "There are ten kids. I broke the list down by gender and Jen's guesses on sizes."

Sasha looked over the list and nodded. "No problem. Should take me about an hour or two. Dov will be up from his nap in a few minutes and then we'll head out."

"Can I come?" Max asked.

Sasha opened her mouth, then closed it, looking at Kati. "Well, that's up to your mom."

"Um, I don't know…" Kati said.

"You should go too, Kati," Laney said. "Maybe you guys could get some dinner."

Yoni rubbed his stomach. "Well if dinner is involved, I'm going, too."

"And I'll send along a couple of guards. They've been wanting to get away from the grounds," Laney added, trying to sound casual.

Kati looked at Laney, and Laney could read the indecision on her friend's face.

"It'll be okay," Laney urged. "And it'll good for Max."

Kati kept her eyes on Laney for a long minute before nodding. "Okay. Sounds good."

Laney smiled. "Bring me back something, would you?"

"Hamburger and fries?" Sasha asked.

Laney smiled. "Perfect."

The group trooped out of the office and Laney let out a sigh, wishing she could go with them and just relax for a few hours.

Instead she pulled over a stack of resumes for the psychologists they were considering interviewing. Her uncle, Patrick Delaney, had been pinch-hitting as a counselor, and had been doing a fine job, but they all knew that with the problems some of these kids would be dealing with, they would require professional help.

"Okay, Dr. Shields, what do you bring to the table?"

She spent the next hour going through the files. Finally she stood up and stretched. Cleo raised her head expectantly.

Laney smiled as she shrugged on her jacket. "Okay. A quick walk. And then back to work."

Cleo got to her feet, kneading her claws on the carpet as she stretched.

Laney shook her head and added a carpet to the list of things she'd need to have replaced.

But then she smiled. In the grand scheme of things, if her biggest worries involved carpeting and beds, she was doing all right. In fact, she could most definitely get used to this.

Check out The Belial Children on Amazon Today!

ACKNOWLEDGMENTS

First and foremost, I must thank my family. Lou being attacked in the park was the first scene I wrote for *The Belial Children*. As I went along though I knew that I was trying to cram too much into one book. Lou was the story line that could be removed without changing the book. But I really liked Lou. So I decided to give Lou her own book.

Then the other problem cropped up: Lou's story needed to be told before *The Belial Children*. So it was a rush to the finish to get both books out at the same time.

My family's support is the only reason that I was able to get both done on schedule. My husband was a godsend and my kids were very good about respecting the door being closed to my office. Thank you guys for all your help with these books and for just making my life a happier place. You are my greatest gifts.

Thank you to all the people who helped with getting this book out. Thank you to Damonza for your incredible work on the cover. I absolutely love it!

Thank you to my editorial crew - Elizabeth McCartan, David Gatewood, and Taewan. I appreciate all your hard work.

ABOUT THE AUTHOR

Author, Criminologist, Terrorism Expert, Jeet Kune Do Black Sash, Runner, Dog Lover.

Amazon best-selling author R.D. Brady writes supernatural and science fiction thrillers. Her thrillers include ancient mysteries, unusual facts, non-stop action, and fierce women with heart.

Prior to beginning her writing career, RD Brady was a criminologist who specialized in life-course criminology and international terrorism. She's lectured and written numerous academic articles on the genetic influence on criminal behavior, factors that influence terrorist ideology, and delinquent behavior formation.

After visiting counter-terrorism units in Israel, RD returned home with a sabbatical in front of her and decided to write that book she'd been thinking about. Four years later she left academia with the publication of her first book, *The Belial Stone*, and hasn't looked back.

To learn about her upcoming publications, sign up for her newsletter here or on her website (rdbradybooks.com).

Copyright © 2014 by R.D. Brady

The Belial Recruit: A Belial Series Novella

ASIN (E-Book): B00P39H9CU

ISBN (Paperback): 979-8748841078

ISBN (Hardcover): 9798797921615

Published by Scottish Seoul Publishing, LLC, Dewitt, NY

All Rights Reserved. No part of this book may be reproduced or transmitted in any form or by any means, electronic or mechanical, including photocopying, recording, or by any information storage and retrieval system without the written permission of the author, except where permitted by law.

Printed in the United States of America.

BOOKS BY R.D. BRADY

Hominid

The Belial Series (in order)
    The Belial Stone
    The Belial Library
    The Belial Ring
    Recruit: A Belial Series Novella
    The Belial Children
    The Belial Origins
    The Belial Search
    The Belial Guard
    The Belial Warrior
    The Belial Plan
    The Belial Witches
    The Belial War
    The Belial Fall
    The Belial Sacrifice

The Belial Rebirth Series
    The Belial Rebirth
    The Belial Spear

The Belial Restored
The Belial Blood
The Belial Angel
The Belial Templar (Coming Soon)

The A.L.I.V.E. Series
B.E.G.I.N.
A.L.I.V.E.
D.E.A.D.
R.I.S.E.
S.A.V.E.

The H.A.L.T. Series
Into the Cage
Into the Dark *(Coming soon)*

The Steve Kane Series
Runs Deep
Runs Deeper

The Unwelcome Series
Protect
Seek
Proxy

The Nola James Series
Surrender the Fear
Escape the Fear
Tackle the Fear
Return the Fear

The Gates of Artemis Series
The Key of Apollo
The Curse of Hecate
The Return of the Gods

R.D. BRADY WRITING AS SADIE HOBBES

The Demon Cursed Series
    Demon Cursed
    Demon Revealed
    Demon Heir

The Four Kingdoms
    Order of the Goddess

Be sure to sign up for R.D.'s mailing list to be the first to hear when she has a new release!

Printed in Great Britain
by Amazon